The PLAYHOUSE

Elaine Ford

McGRAW-HILL BOOK COMPANY

New York   St. Louis   San Francisco
Düsseldorf   Mexico
London   Toronto   Sydney

2 3 4 5 6 7 8 9 BP BP 8 7 6 5 4 3 2 1 0

LIBRARY OF CONGRESS CATALOGING IN PUBLICATION DATA

Ford, Elaine.
The playhouse.
I. Title.
PZ4.F694Pl [PS3556.O697] 813'.54 80-10928
ISBN 0-07-021503-0

Book design by Roberta Rezk

For Mark,
Geoffrey, Lisa,
Andrew, and Annebeth

1

I am a tall girl. I have a round face, pale as skim milk; my mouth is bluish as though stained with ink. My ears have an extra margin of cartilage where they are connected to my head, forcing them slightly outward. Jug-ears, Gran calls them, my inheritance from my father. I brush my hair, standing at Gran's bureau in the hall. It is short hair, straight and shaggy around the ears. Might as well be honestly ugly: I'll never make my mark in the world with my looks.

I let myself through the chain-link fence gate, clanking the bar shut behind me to keep Pat's dog in. Verdun Street. The sidewalk is broken in places where the maple roots have grown too fat underneath and have been patched with cement or tar; it is edged with weeds and beer cans and torn bits of newspaper.

It is early summer and so there are mysterious diggings in some of the yards, piles of sledgehammered brick

Elaine Ford

mixed with dirt—abortive efforts at home improvement. Someone has been repainting the shutters and window-sills of his house, but has stopped where the ladder ended or the paint ran out. In another yard a few infant tomato plants, tied to strings, straggle vainly toward the sun. Already the branches overhead are thick and interlaced, and even weeds do not thrive very well.

The house on the corner has a retired washing machine left casually in the yard, its back nakedly exposed. That's the house all the old ladies on the street cluck over. Because people do for themselves, keep to themselves, keep up their property as best they can—this landlord sins against them. They have no way to get even since he doesn't even live there, just collects the rent. What can you expect? Gran says. He even had the yard blacktopped for parking, not a stick of grass growing in it.

An old man is contemplating his dog defecate under the concrete bleachers; otherwise, the athletic field is empty. The arc lights switch on over the basketball courts, darkening the tangle of bushes behind. Pat is no doubt playing basketball or is somewhere in the knot of onlookers, smoking a cigarette, but I don't bother to look that way. Rock music blasts out of the teen center on the other side of the field. The old man's dog, rat-faced and grinning, comes racing after me, yapping and scratching at my dress with its paws.

Things like that are always happening. Once one of the mental patients slapped me, raising a great hand-shaped welt on my cheek, and her doctor told me that I had somehow invited the attack. I still don't understand it, but this old man has the same idea; he calls the dog lovingly and it trots away, the injured party.

I'm early. To kill time I go into the grocery store on the corner of Massachusetts Avenue. On the partitioned stand are peaches, not yet ripe. "First of the season," the clerk remarks, dropping some into a paper bag. They sound like stones. Gran would say, "Picked out of season, poison the liver," but then, Gran could find some fault in any saint you might mention, never mind sour fruit. Through the paper they have a solid, satisfying feel.

Turn right on Mass Av, toward Porter Square. Past the rug remnant store, the Chinese laundry, the discount toy store crammed with remaindered doll carriages, the dry cleaner, the shop that used to sell electrical appliances but is now vacant except for corrugated bulb cartons in the window.

The shopfronts end and are replaced by a hedge which has raged out of control, thrusting its prickly branches in all directions. The new growth is pale delicate green and vigorous. I've been behind this house many times, deep in the uncut grass and orchard, but never inside the house itself. It is large, unplanned, decayed—an oversight. If we had not been used to the house standing there in the midst of business premises, I suppose we would have thought it foolish. But children do not like changes.

I yank the bell-pull, a piece of knotted wire dangling out of a hole on the door frame. Perhaps it's not the bell-pull at all, I think, since no one answers: only the frayed end of some fixture that's been torn away. The house is dark and quiet.

But then Dr. Glass opens the door. He lays his large brown hand for a moment on my shoulder. "I'm glad you decided to come." We go up. The steps are thickly padded with carpeting; the oak panels lining the stairwell are the color of pulled taffy.

At the top of the house is the sickroom. A library really, converted with the addition of an iron cot, some metal basins, a medicine cabinet on casters. The room smells strongly of rubbing alcohol.

Charlie O'Clair sits in a reclining chair, one of those old-fashioned push-chairs with wicker sides and back and heavy useless wheels. He smiles, gesturing toward the bandaged leg: a casual flicking of fingers both dismissing it and explaining why he can't rise to greet me. "She's young, Abe." In his left cheek is an indentation which seems not so much a dimple as a scar, because it doesn't fade when the smile stops.

"She can do the job."

"I told you I don't need anybody. Out of the cradle or not."

"Of course not, Charlie. Only until the suture heals." Dr. Glass is laying equipment from the cabinet out on the bed table. "I'll show Maureen how I want the dressing changed. Give me the leg."

The incision is neat and dime-sized, oozing a little clear fluid. Looks like nothing much. Routine. The patient is restless, though, picking at the cuffs of his dressing gown.

"Any problems, Maureen?"

Again Mr. O'Clair says, "She's too young. What does she know?"

But the doctor ignores him and looks at me. "Any worries about that little cut?"

"No."

"All right." He goes into the adjoining bathroom to wash his hands. I feel foolish standing there, holding the bag of peaches and thinking about how that old man's dog has soiled my dress.

"Abe Glass a friend of yours?" Charlie O'Clair's voice is high-pitched and has an irritating brassy quality.

"He took out my grandmother's gallbladder."

"Ah." Abruptly he laughs. "Well, don't worry. You won't be needed here for long."

Dr. Glass chooses the front table in a diner a few blocks away from the O'Clair house. Across the street the Ford showroom is closing, turning off its inner lights. The waitress wipes our table in slow, thoughtful, artistic swirls. "Two coffees—and a couple of slices of cheesecake," Dr. Glass tells her. She wanders off behind the counter, tucking her sausage curls into a hairnet.

"Cheesecake—to clog up my mouth so I can't say no?"

"What do you mean, no?"

"I don't want this job. I have other plans."

"Like what?"

"I told you. The mental hospital."

"And you'll earn enough to keep yourself in paper clips."

I say low and deliberately, "You know it's not for the money."

"You're right, I know you. You like a tough fight."

"Oh, fine. I can be Charlie O'Clair's private punching bag."

"He's dying, Maureen."

I am silent, skeptical, cutting my cheesecake into squares.

"I put him in the hospital a week ago. Tumor on the right leg, just below the knee. Malignant melanoma. I could have taken off the leg—but what's the point? Damn fool let it go so long it's surely in the groin by now, anyway. Spreads like wildfire to all those nodes. So I just cut it out, the primary site."

"The papers say he's running for City Council this year."

5

"Even in North Cambridge, death supersedes politics."

I smile ruefully.

"There's not much scut work involved, not now at least. You saw the situation yourself."

"I suppose so."

"Look, Maureen—Charlie's a good friend. He helped me through a bad patch a few years ago. Well, I won't go into that." I remember what he's referring to, though. A malpractice suit involving the puncturing of a sciatic nerve with a hypodermic needle, not his fault but he nearly got nailed for it, and it put a big scare into everybody at the hospital. Charlie O'Clair worked with the lawyer who eventually got him off. "Anyway, I'd feel a lot better if there were somebody in that house I could trust."

"What about his wife?"

"The truth is I don't know her very well. But I'd guess she's not up to it, the emotional support. She doesn't want him to know the diagnosis—she's frightened or stubborn—I don't know. A mistake, of course. Charlie's going to figure out pretty soon that something's up."

"That's quite a burden you put on me."

He leans over his pipe to pack it with tobacco. His shiny tanned head is clipped almost to his skull in back. He looks up and smiles. "I knew you'd do it."

2

I cut the meat off the bone, handling it gingerly with my short, square-tipped fingers. It is still hot from the soup pot. The knife is dull; wiping my hand on the seat of my blue jeans, I pick through the open utensil drawer, looking for the whetstone. Nothing is ever where it's supposed to be in this house.

The kitchen is hot, the air heavy with the smell of boiling lamb. Walls, cupboards, chairs: everything in this room is the graceless color known as Landlady Green, painted dozens of times over peeling paint so that every surface is bumpy and crazed, all those old times showing right through. One knot is fallen out of a cupboard door, making a kind of comical eye and the grain of the wood a perpetually astonished eyebrow over it.

Gran sits at the kitchen table, playing cards and drinking endless cups of milky tea. She blows her nose loudly. Through the window she can see the railroad tracks, the section of the Boston and Maine that divides North Cambridge from the rest of the city. Somebody ought to cut down those weeds along the track, she says; they're what give her the hay fever every June. She'd call the Council about it, but that no-good Kelly would probably tell her the weeds belong to the B & M, not the city. You couldn't ever win.

"You come in with Pat last night?"

"No." I hack at the lamb bone.

"I thought I heard you come in together."

"No."

She sighs, washing her hands of me. I miss every chance.

"I went to interview for a job at the O'Clair house."

Gran shuffles. It is an old deck, soft and flabby, some of the corners inadvertently marked, but Gran is not too proud to take advantage. Though her curiosity is prickled she continues to slap the cards down on the table: two face down, five face up, two face down, five face up.

"O'Clair, the lawyer?"

"Yes."

"So she's worn him down at last."

I take a couple of potatoes out of the bin. They've begun to root, I notice. "I didn't say he was worn down. Little nick taken out of his leg."

"I knew he'd be sorry—marrying her."

"It's nothing to do with his wife."

"I was a guest at her christening." Gran's face, powdered thick as a cake, cracks with disgust. "But do you think she notices me now? Driving around in that big black Buick, she wouldn't give me a lift from the trolley stop if I fell down dead in the street."

"You wouldn't care then, I guess."

"She's plain mean, and that's the whole of it."

"Maybe she's lonely."

"You bet she's lonely. If you don't do for other people, there's nobody going to do for you."

I cut around the potato sprouts with the tip of the peeler. I think about the giving and receiving of favors: Dr. Glass returning O'Clair's. The whole political process working like that. And Charlie O'Clair's wife somehow left out of it.

I hurt her once. She was coming into church for Mass with her husband; it was the Sunday before Easter and everybody carrying crosses made of palm leaves. They couldn't find seats and I touched his arm and said, "There is a seat for your mother." Her face was soft and lined and she wore a hat with pale-green flowers. She pretended not to hear me.

Gran pours more tea. "They thought she was going to be an old maid, but then he married her. He was living in her father's house, a boarder. You know, he didn't come from around here."

"Maybe she wouldn't look so old if she had children."

"Well, she did have one, at that. Must be twenty years ago at least. People said it wasn't born right, and she had it sent away to a home."

"Not born right?"

"I never saw it, of course. They took it away direct from the hospital, and people don't tell you things like that right out."

I imagine a tiny, thick-necked infant, wrapped so its face wouldn't be seen.

"She never had another. You can't blame her for that—maybe there was something wrong with her." Gran stops turning over the cards and watches the commuter train out of Boston rattle past, through the high grass behind the sewer-pipe yard. Her thoughts shift to something else: my mother, perhaps.

"I took the job, though, Gran."

"I don't know why he married her, I swear I don't. People do strange things."

The place where I have lived with my grandmother, almost all my life, is a narrow two-family house on Verdun Street, across from a rug-cleaning company and a sewer-pipe yard. The house is covered with brown asphalt siding, two-tone, decorated with a honeycomb pattern that always makes me think of filled sugar-wafer cookies, obscuring goodness knows what infelicity or decay. There is a small yard for hanging clothes enclosed by a deciduous hedge, and next to it a tangled patch of lilac and pussy willows where Cissy and I used to play. A rusty tricycle is hidden there now.

Behind the stoneware yard—a garden of clay sewer pipes of various shapes laid in formal rows—are the railroad tracks, the Boston and Maine. Next to the foot tunnel under the tracks is a factory smokestack, a round brick tower, silent now. The factory was once a paper mill. It is no longer being used and the windows are gone as though pecked out by birds. In the tunnel are broken beer bottles, amber and green shards mixed with cinder, and grass which grows mysteriously, without sunlight or soil.

The houses on Verdun Street were never meant to be gracious. They were built cheaply after the beginning of the century, deliberately squeezing the affairs of two or three families under one roof, the rooms small and dark, the closets shallow. But still respectable, decent. The maples along the street have grown up, entirely on their own initiative, giving the street—especially in summer—a certain feeling of isolated calm, deeply shaded. It is different here from the next block, where construction of the new school and the basketball courts have opened up barren sunny fields.

Number 19–21 has a slightly prolapsed balcony, supported by a glassed-in porch. A string of Christmas lights, empty of their bulbs, decorates the porch in all seasons.

Our landlady lives below us. She is a divorcée, a large, generous, nosy person with hair so bleached and otherwise worked over it is like spun glass. Her husband was an electrician, but he left so long ago I hardly remember him. Pat Meaghan is her son.

In the spring and fall Mrs. Meaghan sits on the old upholstered sofa under the porch windows, knitting and keeping a backward glance on the neighbors. In the summer she goes to stay with her sister, who has a summer cottage near Shrewsbury. The porch is then empty, except for a row of derelict Easter plants on the windowsill, dead stalks still in ribbons and gold foil.

I hardly see Pat now. For the last three years I've been leaving the house before six in time to research my patients' diseases; the morning shift begins at seven. In the evenings when he got home from work I'd be already upstairs, studying. And then he'd be out again, playing ball under the arc lamps at the MDC courts.

I try to avoid him because of the way he accidentally touches me if we pass next to the mailboxes on the porch. His pale hair is combed smoothly over his high forehead. There's something wrong with the light switch in the back hall and he's supposed to fix it, but he never gets around to it. He's careless; he leaves things scattered. Hockey skates with rusted blades, ball pumps.

In Gran's bureau, in a candy box full of catechism cards and school reports, there is a snapshot of Pat, with a

Band-Aid on his chin, pushing me in my baby carriage. He is wearing shorts. My face is fat-cheeked, surrounded by a ruffled bonnet, as round-eyed as my lucite Minnie Mouse. In the background my mother, wearing a striped dress with padded shoulders, sits on the wood steps. Those steps have by now decayed and been replaced with concrete. Also, the small foundation bushes in the picture have grown up unpruned and press against the porch window. Pat's grin is the same, though, off-center and indiscriminate.

One time I was reading on the porch sofa. Pat came in through the screen door. He made a grab for the book; I knew he'd read some part of it out loud in a sappy way to tease me. His name for me was "Worm," short for "Bookworm." We tussled over it and then suddenly he kissed my mouth. He felt my newly erupted breast, too, through my shirt. We were very quiet; we heard Gran stomping around on the upstairs balcony, hanging out the wash.

I have not thought about that kiss for long time.

I am putting away the supper dishes. There is an invasion of fruit flies in the kitchen, darting in front of my eyes like the dots signifying consternation in a cartoon. They are too tiny to catch. I pull the light cord over the sink and stand in the dark, eating one of my peaches. The flesh is tough and sour, coming away clean from the pit.

In the glare of the streetlight I see Pat and a girl coming in the chain-link fence gate. They leave it swinging. The girl has shiny teased hair, black as though shoeblacked, and plucked eyebrows the shape of toenail clippings. Pat's hand touches the girl's neck.

Quietly I open the door in the upstairs hall and go down the cold cracked linoleum steps. My feet are bare.

From the lowest stair I can see them through the glass pane in the door. They sit on the sofa talking, flicking ash from their cigarettes onto the dirty floor. Pat's dog, locked inside the house, hears them and scratches insistently on the door, but they pay no attention. Finally the girl presses the two butts into the dry soil of one of the tulip pots on the sill. She laughs. She shifts her soft body to lie under him.

I feel the peach pit, hard and convoluted, still in my hand.

3

I boil water on the hotplate in Charlie O'Clair's
room, the six-sided white room at the top of the
house. I pour water over a teabag in a china cup that has
been sent up from the kitchen, twirl the teabag by the
string so that the amber infusion soaks out into the water.
When the tea is nearly black I lift out the bag and float a
thin slice of lemon on top. Milk and sugar are for babies
and the immigrant Irish, he says. The kettle hisses on the
hotplate, which pops as it cools.

"The house *and* the contents," he is saying into the
phone. "No, damn it, the house *and* the contents." The
teacup rattles in the saucer. He gives a quick smile. "Well,
let me talk to the agent, then."

Bored, I look around. His narrow iron cot is covered
with a white muslin spread. Over the floor boards are an-
cient tacked-down straw mats, edged in black. They have
clearly been there since the house was built, but they still

smell faintly of grass, intensifying the smell of tea rising from his cup.

The windows are without curtains. Between them are bookshelves, half filled with an odd assortment of philosophy and history texts, camping guides, old novels in no particular order. Their spines are broken and faded; I wonder whether they belong to Charlie O'Clair or were simply left there when Old Man Morris died. Hanging from the ceiling is an inoperative gas fixture from which the cream-colored paint is peeling, showing black underneath.

The sixth wall has two doors, one leading to the stairs, the other opening into a white-tiled bathroom. I rinse out his cup and saucer in the sink, just for something to do. The bathtub is raised on splayed lion feet. Against the frosted window, gauze curtains hang without moving; the window is shut and the air is still. His denture soaks in a glass. This room, even more than the other, gives the impression of age, of past use, of suspended listening.

His wound is sutured but raw-looking, under the sterile gauze. I wear a paper mask over my mouth and nose. With the forceps I arrange a new dressing over the incision. He winces. "These are just the odds and ends, the discards up here." He talks as though continuing an interrupted conversation. "I'm trapped in this old room."

Unhooking the mask from behind my ears, I tell him, "I like this room. I like old things."

But he has picked up a book and unfolded his eyeglasses. I find his preoccupation unsettling; I'd almost prefer the hostility he showed at first—then I might be able to communicate. That's supposed to be my job.

I make his bed, tight with fresh linen, and arrange the medication in a fluted paper cup: pain killer, tranquilizer, antibiotic. Three brown jars in a neat row in the medicine cabinet, like the three wise monkeys in Gran's sitting room: see no evil, hear no evil, speak no evil. I feel an impulse to chant the words out loud, to break the silence. Or I could say, "You are going to die, Charlie O'Clair, think on that."

But I am a wise monkey. I spend my time straightening the books in his shelves until finally he looks up, annoyed.

"There's no reason for you to stay any longer."

"I'm supposed to stay until five."

"I'm sure no one will object. Go along."

I unpin my cap, tuck it into a plastic bag. The stairs, covered in thick plush carpet, mottled blue and green, are completely silent under my hard white shoes.

Before opening the oak door, I pause for a moment. On the wall is a group of framed snapshots and newspaper clippings. Charlie O'Clair is accepting a letter of appreciation from the Heart Fund, standing next to Tip O'Neill at an Eighth Congressional District banquet, giving a speech to the Jaycees, dancing an Irish jig. I find it hard to connect the chalk-faced man upstairs with this laughing public person.

It is raining. From the windows at the top of the house I can see two Romanesque towers, one to the north, the other to the northwest, as though I inhabit some no-man's-land between two city-states. The nearer tower, St. John's, is made of chocolate brown brick, inlaid with green and red mosaic, trimmed with ivory stone, its pillars candy-striped. The other, the French church, is the color of sand. It is less decorated, like a church built in a remote desert land of local materials.

Cars splash by in the street below.

I wander to another window. I can see the flat tarred

roof over the dry cleaner, the carpet store; the signs, streaked with rust, swing in the wind. Flats of petunias in front of the grocery are waterlogged. An orange trolley consumes an old lady into its flapping, collapsing doors.

The air conditioner in the window hums, a row of condensation droplets collecting along its lip. Here it is like waiting at the dentist, the boredom worse than the pain.

He never looks at me. His voice is high for a man's and quick to cut me off. He holds out his hand for a cup of tea; he sucks in his breath silently when I care for his wound. He obediently swallows the tablets, holds the thermometer under his tongue, and brushes his teeth, spitting into the stainless-steel basin. He clicks the two-tooth denture into his mouth. A fight—or decay? I wonder. His body is tightly wrapped in a maroon silk robe. Whiskey, also, he takes as if by prescription, at room temperature from a plain shot glass.

He holds a book but does not turn the pages rapidly; I scarcely hear them turn. I finger the bandage scissors in my pocket.

He telephones his secretary. She's out on the Cape, on vacation, and the office is closed. But he's remembered some detail about a pending contract and has her paged all over the grounds of the hotel until her voice, grating and defensive, comes out of the receiver.

"You dropped the ball, Grace."

He listens to her with his eyes closed, his index finger curled against his cheek, the teeth biting the middle finger. His hair is stippled with gray. He must be—what?—forty at least. The mark in his cheek deepens as he considers his course of action, and that tiny movement in his face suggests power. And yet I feel something vulnerable in the tension.

"All right. I'll get someone here to manage it."

His eyes open suddenly before he replaces the telephone; he catches my stare. "True, your friend Abe Glass has locked me out of my office. However, I happen to have another key." He writes something on a memo pad and tears the page off, leaving a ragged edge. The key is cold in my hand.

The last thing I want to do is ape that woman's shrillness, though I am annoyed, because he has me outwitted. Bed rest makes no sense if he's not really sick, and that's the line we're all giving him. Well, so far as I'm concerned he can fiddle around with contracts until he croaks.

I walk down two flights, past the closed, quiet doors on the second floor. The varnished oak banister is wide and smooth; the steps are unlighted except for the stained-glass window on the lower landing. The house has a pervasive sweet smell, almost like ether. Furniture polish, perhaps.

In the formal drawing room there is a grand piano and a medallioned Oriental carpet. The bright-red color of the carpet is so fresh, it might just have been unrolled. The draperies are drawn. All the furniture is protected with fitted clear plastic covers, in case some feckless client straggles in by mistake, I suppose.

Across the hall is his office, a bare and ordinary room dominated by a long table and mismatched chairs. I cough. The room is stuffy, windows shut tight and the air conditioner unplugged. Wet leaves of a tree-of-heaven tree slap against the outside of the window.

On the desk I notice a silver-framed photograph of a young woman with soft features and long hair drawn back from her forehead who must be his wife of twenty years ago. Next to it is a small plant in a chipped clay pot. No one has remembered to water it; some of the leaves have yellowed and fallen.

I find the right folder in the filing cabinet. Surprising, his handwriting on the slip of yellow paper. A tight, bunched-up backhand, not the brash scrawl I would have expected.

Just before locking the door, I pick up the plant and carry it to the back of the house. Nobody is in the kitchen, though the screen door has been propped open and there is an unfolded newspaper on the table. Someone has been pasting trading stamps into a booklet. The radio, untuned and crackling with static, plays a heavy late-afternoon symphony. I hold the plant under the tap and let the water trickle into it, feeling unaccountably sad at the futility of the gesture.

4

Cissy and I used to go to the playhouse together although she wasn't allowed to: trespassing was a sort of venial sin. Her mother was always telling her what she was allowed and what she wasn't. Gran never said anything like that to me. I was just expected to know. In some ways I envied Cissy; the only rules I could break were my own.

The playhouse was hidden in the weeds behind Old Man Morris' house, between the back garden and the orchard that crowded up next to his property line. The fact of its existence was passed from child to child in the neighborhood, the same way we learned riddles, insults, jump-rope chants. Boys went there to smoke; we'd find their crumpled cigarette packages inside the cupboards. The playhouse was leaky and needed paint even then, the cupboard doors warped, the floor boards rotting. I'm not sure why Cissy and I went there. Perhaps it was the decay that attracted us, the air of ruin.

"Is the kettle on?"

I fill the kettle in the bathroom. If the playhouse hasn't been torn down, I ought to be able to see the roof from this window, behind the gauze curtains and frosted glass. Idly, I wonder whether Charlie O'Clair has been inside or even knows it's there. He wasn't a child in this neighborhood.

The hotplate ring glows red.

A strange tree grew over the playhouse, with slender pods a foot long dangling down against the casement windows. The tree's name, I found out later, is catalpa, but we called it the bean tree. You couldn't eat those beans; you had to pretend.

The kettle has a lisping whistle, dying slowly as the ring cools. I brew the tea and put the cup on the table by his chair. As usual he doesn't look up from his reading. He mashes the lemon into the tea with a spoon and blows across the rim of the cup, still absorbed in his book.

I go back to the bathroom and raise the window. Yes, the bulbous white roof is there, showing through the leaves of the catalpa tree. When I see Cissy I'll tell her that I am now mistress of the playhouse. Well, not exactly—but she'll enjoy the joke.

As I stand there, a black car moves around the curved driveway, crunching pebbles under the tires. Abruptly, it stops. Mrs. O'Clair gets out of the car and calls to someone I can't see, because of the limits of the window frame.

"Where do you think you're going? This is private property."

She stands in her puddly yard, a short, sharp-nosed person in an accordion-pleated plastic rain hat. She has a very small mouth and a chin full of a number of strange puckers. The car runs in neutral, gently shuddering.

"Listen to me, you don't understand. There are snakes in that field, poisonous snakes."

Elaine Ford

The child must have run away, because she parks the car in the garage and disappears into the house. In a few moments she returns with a bucket of soapy water and a wood-backed bristle brush. Now I see that there are muddy footprints on the concrete apron in front of the garage. She stoops. In her gray tailored coat, with silver buttons down the back that don't button anything, she scrubs away at the stains. She wipes her eye with her coat sleeve; ammonia fumes from the bucket, probably, are making her eyes tear.

Again, rain is tossed against the window glass like handfuls of tacks. I sit by the north window, reading aloud from Thucydides. The stiffness of my new uniform makes me feel formal and constrained; I can taste dust in my mouth.

He is experiencing more pain in the bad leg now. He lies on the narrow cot, his back raised by a bank of pillows, his eyes hidden behind a dark-veined hand. I read about the funeral preparations for the slain Athenian soldiers, the oration of Pericles over their bones, the laying waste of Attica. The church bells strike the quarter hour.

I rise to check the amount of bleeding from the incision. The dark blood is thickly clotted, but serous matter seeps from the edge. Black stubble is returning to his leg after surgery. I clean the dried blood on his calf with alcohol; he tenses away from me.

"In case you wonder, I don't read Thucydides just to decorate my mind."

I tuck the top sheet under the mattress, leaving a pleat for foot room. His eyes, deep in their sockets, are very pale blue and he squints as though the light hurts them. I wait for him to explain.

"For example, patriotism can be a useful tool."

I shake out the bedspread and tuck that in too.

"But I suppose Thucydides bores you."

"I like the ships, the old stone walls."

"That's right, you said you like old things."

Surprising that he remembered that.

"What do you like about them?"

I shrug. "They last. People don't."

"That's a cynical thing to say."

"So is what you said about patriotism."

He laughs. "You're right." Quietly, he says, "You're not like my wife. She hates old things. She took one look at this house and called in a horde of cleaners to scrape it all out." It is a disturbing image, like the taking of a curette to a uterus. "Then the decorators came and filled it up again. Cost a pile. Would you have done that, Maureen?"

That's the first time he's called me by my Christian name. "I don't have a pile to spend."

He sleeps, and I pick up the mending I have brought with me: a blouse of Gran's that has come unstitched in the armpit. Her fingers are too arthritic now for sewing. After a while he startles me by saying, "So houses last and people don't."

"I was thinking about my own family."

"And what about them?"

He is an irritating man; this sudden concentration on me is as disturbing as his previous silence.

"My father died in Belgium in 1944, my mother later in an asylum. I've gotten used to the fact that people are . . . impermanent."

"Was your father killed in the war?"

I rethread the needle and pull the knot tight before answering. "His body was never found, never identified. He was listed as missing in action. So there was always this fantasy that he might come home. He never did, of course."

"Is it painful for you?"

"No. Sometimes I imagine him in some Belgian village, an old deserter, father of a bunch of jug-eared children. It was hard on my mother, though, his disappearing like that."

"She talked to you about him."

"She was in the mental hospital. When my grandmother visited her, I had to wait outside."

"Why?"

"I guess because she was out of her head so much, and they thought I'd be scared. She was in a locked ward, and they'd lock the door behind my grandmother when she went in. Still, I wish I'd known her, even the way she was."

"It's sometimes better not to try to hide things, even from children. They always find out, some way."

"Yes. I like things to be honest."

"But there are some people who aren't as strong as they ought to be, who can't take it. Situations are always more complicated than you imagine."

I suppose he's thinking of his wife now. "Maybe."

When I give him his back rub his muscles relax under my hands for the first time, because of this confession.

I begin to remember things I've kept tightly locked away, ever since the summer my mother died.

We played Monopoly all that afternoon on the porch, Pat and I; Gran had gone out somewhere. We sat on the cool linoleum while flies buzzed hopelessly against the screen door. I was eleven. Pat taunted me when I made a mistake; he could get away with it, since he was five years older and condescending to play with me. His mother brought us lemonade in a rinsed-out milk bottle.

Before the game was finished, Gran came back with a priest. The three of us walked to a brick building which was at the top of a great flight of concrete steps. Perhaps it is the same funeral home as the one I can see from Charlie O'Clair's window; I'm not sure. The priest explained to me that my mother had died and the coffin was going to be sealed, but that I must say goodbye to her first.

They prayed: Hail Mary, full of grace, the Lord is with thee. I couldn't see anything for a long time except for the pattern of whirling white and red roses on the carpet, and the priest's shiny black shoes under his soutane, and my grandmother's brown shoes with the spattering of air holes in the splayed sides. The taste of lemon coated my mouth. At last someone pushed me forward to the edge of the coffin.

That is the memory I have of my mother. She was dressed in a beige crepe nightgown with long sleeves covering her hands and a collar of lace at her neck. Her hair was long and black, threaded with gray, and I could see bald spots in it that whoever had brushed it had not been able to hide. Her face was the pale color of cheese, except for a network of broken blood vessels in her cheeks. But the worst thing was the baldness—what had caused it? Had she pulled out her own hair for some reason I could not imagine?

I wonder now whether it was before or after my mother died that Pat fondled me on the porch sofa. I wonder how much he knew.

Charlie O'Clair is pulling all these thoughts out of me like kapok out of a stuffed toy. I must be more careful. It is not as though he is the first dying patient I ever cared for.

I wait in a molded plastic chair at the coin-op laundry, listening to the machines crank from cycle to cycle, out of step with each other. Their inner cogs grind. There is always shifty-eyed competition to get at the machines, people pushing ahead of turn, and since no dryers are free I straddle my tub of wet wash, ready to make a dash. The place smells of electrical short and ammonia. Two small boys chase each other, tripping over the legs of old men.

I am mulling over a dream, the kind you wake up with in the morning and are haunted by all day. In the dream I sit in the drawing room in the O'Clair house, with the blood-red carpet spread before me. Everything, including the piano, is covered in plastic wrap. Mrs. O'Clair sits beside me on the encapsulated damask sofa; she wears a quilted dressing gown, silvery; it does not strike me as strange that she should be dressed in asbestos padding. Leaning casually against the wall on my side of the sofa is a pay telephone booth which is not hooked up. I ask why it is there. "Oh, I ordered it when Charlie was here, because he makes so many long-distance calls. But of course the telephone company didn't deliver it until after he was gone. I guess that should teach me a lesson."

Does gone mean died? And what is the lesson?

Monday morning, the church bells striking nine. With some shyness I hand Charlie O'Clair the parcel I have brought; it is wrapped in tissue paper but with the outlines plain enough to see, spout and handle. His fingers fumble at the bits of tape. A teapot, white, with the design of a stylized Chinese garden in blue, an ornamental garden pavilion and a feathery willow tree.

His face is without definable expression.

"I'm afraid the spout is a bit chipped. I saw it in the window of Max Keezer's and I thought, well, I can make a better cup of tea with that. Teabags really aren't very good."

Apropos of nothing he says, "I once gave my wife a canary on her birthday. She gave it away to somebody; she said it was too much trouble."

"What is your wife like?"

"Oh—she's just a wife."

I can hear in his tightly controlled voice that the pain is worse today.

5

"I should have been a safecracker."
Gowan is behind the television set, unscrewing
the back. He is one of Charlie O'Clair's hangers-on, a
tenor who sings at banquets and rallies, an envelope-
licker, a leg man. He has sparse hair and a face that is narrow and creased, like a mud road after a dozen trucks have
backed and filled over it. I know him slightly. He's a salesman in the shoe store where Pat works and sometimes he
comes around to have a beer with Pat. When he's downstairs, Peggy Meaghan's hoarse voice bellows with laugh-
ter. I guess he knows every joke in the book.

"This set is a regular antique, Charlie. Where'd you
get it?"

Charlie says, straight-faced, "I saw it in the window
at Max Keezer's."

"No kidding. I wouldn't have thought Max would let
just anybody carry off this valuable piece of memora-
bilia."

"I'm not just anybody."

Gowan points the screwdriver at him. "True, Charlie. True."

"Remember the last antique appliance we dealt with?"

"Yeah. Yeah. The washer."

Charlie laughs but Gowan puts on a mournful expression. "Polluting the river, Charlie. And you practically a member of the City Council."

"Not quite."

Gowan looks at me quickly and says, "You hear about the washer, Maureen? No? We were at this dance, in a boathouse on the river. An elegant affair: daffodils on all the tables and professors dancing the cha-cha—made a lot of money for the campaign. Nobody rowdy. But at the end they have a lottery, and this bird Charlie O'Clair wins the jackpot. An old Daisy washer with a wringer and a crank, full of soapy water that's sloshing all over the dance floor. So what does he do?" Gowan by now has an array of tubes spread out over the top of the set and on the floor around him. He points the screwdriver again at Charlie, and it is my instinct to move next to my patient. He's in pain; he doesn't need teasing.

"What he does is enlist *me* in his foul deed. Well, we've had a few Scotches, I admit. We push the washer out the door, down the ramp, and one more heave. Over the side, right into the Charles. It sinks right away, but the soapsuds kind of float on the surface, swirling around, resisting the current."

"That was the ordinary pollution that's always there," Charlie tells me.

"Then down the ramp in their spike heels come the faculty wives. 'He pushed it in, right in the water,' they're all screeching. I put on my best virtuous expression, so they start grabbing at Charlie—his necktie, his coat—and

one big blond gal gets a good hold on him and before anybody knows what's happening, they're both of them in
the drink with the washer."

"*She* floated all right. The frontage on her."

"Admirable," Gowan agrees. "Nothing skimpy
about it."

"Sad in a way she's not a constituent."

"Bad luck."

Gowan is testing the tubes one by one. His hair,
parted so as to hide the bald spot, has fallen down on the
wrong side. He's a funny-looking man but his fingers, as
he says, are sensitive as a safecracker's. "Ah, luck," he
sighs. "That reminds me of Seamus."

"Who is Seamus?" I ask.

"He came to me after my uncle died."

"A relation?"

"A bird. Parrot. He doesn't talk, he tells fortunes;
that's how my uncle made a living. The bird pecked out a
little card with a fortune on it and my uncle pocketed the
quarter and the cop said move on, move on. Well, my
uncle moved on, but Seamus didn't."

Gowan can tell a silly story in a way that touches me.
"Would he tell my fortune, Gowan?"

"I can tell your fortune," Charlie interrupts. I am
standing next to his chair and he takes my hand. He stares
into the palm and runs his index finger very lightly along
the creases. "You have a peasant's hand. Calluses and
blunt square fingers."

I start to draw my hand away, but he hangs on to it.
"No, it's a good hand. There's a special kind of luck in it."
Gowan watches us from behind the television set. We are
all quiet for a moment, and then I move toward the window and Gowan holds a tube.

"Here's the bum one," he says.

"How do you know about television sets?"

"Took a night course in it. I've taken a night course in just about everything."

I think: then what are you doing selling shoes? But I know he's thinking the same thing. He's replacing all the good tubes and Charlie has become bored with the conversation. The restlessness of Charlie's feet under the covers tells me that the pain has returned.

After Gowan packs up his tools and leaves, Charlie says, "Gowan is one of those people who knows everybody but is always alone."

I have now been working in this house two weeks. Charlie is on the phone all afternoon trying to convince the pols that he's still in the running for the Council seat in this ward. I suspect that Mick Gowan has carried the word around about Charlie—the pinched face, the restlessness. Gowan would notice those things.

Though it has been raining the sky is beginning to clear. Birds cry to one another along the electric wires and copper gutters. "They say the weekend's going to be nice."

"What do you do on your weekends?"

"Oh, I read, do the laundry, maybe go to the movies."

"By yourself?"

"I have friends."

He frowns—jealous, I suppose, of my freedom simply to walk down the stairs and out to the street at the end of the day. When I'm ready to go he says shortly, "My wife will make out a check for you."

This arrangement surprises me. I would have expected him to be in charge of financial matters, and up to now his wife has paid no attention to me at all.

Her bedroom door is part way open; she stands at the

window, looking down into the back garden. This room is like the inside of a jewelry box: dim and silk-padded. Because she is so much smaller than I am, I feel clumsy—and a trespasser. She gazes at me for a moment with a soft, clouded expression.

"Oh yes—it's Friday." Her kneehole desk might have been built for a child, a well-organized child. She wears an enameled pin in the shape of an egg on her dress and as she writes the check several gold bracelets click together. I notice that her hands are liver-marked. She fills in the stub and figures out the new balance while I wait. She is careful about detail. Once she made the decision to send away a defective baby. Now I see why it is she who pays the servants.

In the downstairs hall I meet Dr. Glass, who is stopping by on his way home from the hospital.

"Can't you do something with radiation?" I ask.

"Melanomata are nonresponsive to X rays." He looks at me closely. "Have you decided to stick it out?"

"It's going to be a horrible blow when his backers dump him. They're not going to let him run, you know."

"Gradually, he'll stop caring."

"I hope so."

6

I have one uncle, who lives in Watertown. Aside from my grandmother he is my only relative. He was very much older than my father so that the two of them were never close; I think of him as an old man. He never married and he's living on some kind of disability pension, because of his diabetes and because of the confusion in his mind. Sometimes he forgets whether he's given himself the insulin injection or he forgets the rotation. He uses the same needle over and over; he boils it in a little pan. His thighs are full of scars and tough as cowhide. And yet he takes the public transport every day to Newbury Street to play chess. He is a Master.

My uncle Frank Mullen pours me a beer. He keeps his room very neat; he's always prepared to entertain. He has many friends, not only chess players but actors. He belongs to an amateur group that performs locally; he'll be one of a pack of drunks in a barroom scene or a street sweeper with a philosophical bent. My grandmother doesn't approve of him, partly because of his frittered-away life and partly because he is a Mullen. Gran would just as soon forget that any Mullens ever existed.

You don't have to wind up to a conversation with Uncle Frank. He'd only lose concentration during the preamble anyway, so you might as well start off smack dab in the middle.

"Do you remember my mother, Uncle Frank?"

He pokes around in a closet and brings out a framed photograph I've never seen before. It is a formal wedding portrait, and I recognize at once that these young people are my parents. My mother has a cleft in her chin and dark upswept hair under a heavy veil; in the tinted photograph her cheeks look unnaturally flushed. My father is in uniform, his head tilted in a cocky way. One front tooth is slightly awry. His ears stick out frankly below the military haircut. You'd have to trust a person who could let their ears flap in the wind that way and still grin, unembarrassed.

"That's her," Uncle Frank says. He rubs the tarnished brass frame with his coat sleeve. "Of course I remember her. Tim brought her here one time before they were married and I taught her the chess moves. Next time she damn near beat me. Beginner's luck, of course."

"Were you surprised when she had the nervous breakdown?"

"Well—I don't know. She was the kind of person that takes things hard. She couldn't just grieve and then be done with it."

"Because I was around to remind her."

"Oh no, Maureen. You're not blaming yourself."

"I'm just trying to sort out what happened."

Uncle Frank had two toes amputated because of the

diabetes. He walks with a cane, but I think he doesn't really need it; he likes the drama. The cane has a carved head with inset agate eyes and ivory teeth. Uncle Frank says it is an imp out of hell and might get loose some day.

"Am I like her?"

He has always taken me seriously. He thinks about my question for a while before answering. "I don't believe you'd love so . . . fiercely."

His words are peculiarly unsatisfying. I finish my beer and take the trolley back to Verdun Street.

Gran stands in the narrow hallway, looking for something in one of the bureau drawers. Above her head is a luminous bluish painting of the Sacred Heart. "I hear Charlie O'Clair has cancer."

"Who told you that?"

"Mrs. Reilly, who heard it from that colored woman that cooks for him, at the trolley stop."

"They're just guessing, the old gossips."

"You wouldn't deceive me, Maureen?"

I walk under the railroad tracks and past the paper-mill tower. There is a fenced-in field blooming with wild flowers and next to it a scrap-iron yard. I've always been curious about these mysterious iron shapes; it's hard to imagine for what specialized purpose they were pounded out and welded together, and what failure or disaster caused them to be dumped.

I fit my hand through a gap in the wire fence and pick a buttercup.

When my father died he was liberating the port at Antwerp. I've found the town on the map; it is at the end of a long Dutch inlet from the North Sea. I imagine him on the foggy wharf, alone, running, a pain in his lungs, stumbling unseen into the water, pulled down into a black pool. The bright cocky face in the wedding photograph filled with fear, disappearing all in a moment.

It is the loneliness of his death that I think about most, the casual sucking out of his living soul, without notice, without a word from anyone. But I never really knew what happened to him.

Now it is night. A wind has blown up, and there are great clouds in the sky like cotton wads being torn apart. It's much cooler. No stars. A plaster Madonna in one of the yards shines ghostly white; in a house—I don't know whose—a square of calomine-colored light is reflected from the wallpaper.

There are not many streetlights along Middlesex Street, or they are hidden in the thick leaves. The house where Cissy used to live is dark. Someone's rose canes whip in the wind, their tender new leaves crushed against a fence. A dog is barking behind one of the houses.

The potato-chip sign at the end of the street is still il-luminated. I take the road to the right, next to Notre Dame High School and around behind the shrouded nunnery. A child's bicycle has been left on the sidewalk. The moist wind presses my face as though I am breathing into a surgical mask.

All the streets end up here, it seems. I have come to the corner at Massachusetts Avenue where the big house waits, serenely protected from the neon-lit street. The bushes are deep in shadow and the porch light is out, but on the top floor a light is burning. I am sure that it signi-fies pain.

I cut through the hedge and climb the wooden porch stairs. The solid front door is locked, unyielding. I am surprised, but then wonder at my surprise.

It would be unthinkable to pull the bell-wire, to encounter a short, skeptical wife, hair elaborately curled under a nylon cover, armored in a shiny quilted robe. Probably she wouldn't even answer the bell.

Just after me, Pat comes in the gate. The latch clanks shut on the bar. His face is white above his buttoned-up denim jacket; the wind blows his hair back from his forehead. He walks toward me, smoking. I can tell he's had a few beers.

I'm afraid he might try to touch me, but instead he leans against the porch railing. He tosses his cigarette stub into a bush at the far end of the yard and digs his hand under his jacket collar. "My back gets to aching, working in that damn store."

"Everybody complains of back pain."

"Did you notice, I fixed the light for you?"

"The light?"

"The back hall light, it works now. I put a new switch box in the wall. The old one was rusted out."

"Oh yes, I guess I didn't notice. Thanks."

"Gowan tells me he sees you at the O'Clairs'."

"Once or twice."

"Do you like working there?"

"It's all right."

If he wonders where I've been at this hour, he doesn't ask; he goes inside, whistling.

7

s I clean the area around the wound and re-
move the pus-filled gauze, his hand grips my
shoulder. Before laying the fresh dressing on the leg, I
drop my masked cheek against his knuckles, reassuring
him. For a moment I hold the forceps suspended over the
stainless-steel tube of alcohol, then go ahead with the
dressing change. His hand releases me.

He goes through the mail, sorting it into piles for various kinds of action, all of which are put off indefinitely.
He keeps his fingernails pared short. "I've got to get out of
here; I'm going crazy. My hair needs cutting. Is it hot in
the street today?"

"I can cut your hair. I do my own."

He walks with concentration from the cot to the cane
chair, using a crutch and the good leg, refusing my help. I
pin a towel around his shoulders and wait while he parts
his hair. There are pits in his neck where he once had

boils. When he reaches back to hand me the comb, somehow his fingers touch my breast.

"Yes, I'm a fantastic barber—I have all sorts of tricks and talents. Of course, you have curly hair, that's easy to cut. But mine, straight like that, all the mistakes stand right out."

I often see Charlie's wife working in the back garden. She hammers nails into the brick wall and bends and ties the Japanese quince, clips the overblown heads from the roses, pulls weeds. I see her dragging huge branches to a heap she's set aside for burning. She wears a hat that makes her look like a short, squat Mexican.

Charlie's head is bent over his teacup.

"The back garden became very wild when Old Man Morris lived here." I am arranging a branch of the Japanese quince. A thorn jabs my finger and I quickly suck it, to hide the blood from him. But he hasn't noticed.

"Do you ever go there?" I ask him. I am thinking about the playhouse, wondering if his wife has some plan afoot to have it carted away.

"The garden? No. I don't have time."

I pour a second cup of tea for him, feeling the side of the pot to make sure it's still warm. He has changed. The brows seem to straggle out further beyond his eye sockets and his glasses are cutting a crease into the bridge of his nose. Yet the glasses slide down as though greased. He presses the inner corners of his eyes with his thumbs.

"I have a little garden, too. Just ordinary flowers growing along the fence on the side of my house. Pat's dog tries to dig them up; she's determined to bury her bones there, no matter how I try to convince her not to."

"Who is Pat?"

"The landlady's son; they live below us."

I have the impression that he's surprised I know anyone beside himself. Strange how isolated sick people become, and how you have to fight against becoming isolated with them. "Pat's dog is just a skinny brown mutt. Her name's Hilda."

"I'd like to see your garden sometime, Maureen."

I pile the tea things on a tray and carry them to the bathroom to be washed out. I glance down, shy of my own image in the mirror. The wet tea leaves stick to my hands as I empty the pot into the toilet. From the sink I say, "One of these days—I'd love to show it to you."

By now it is July. Charlie is sleeping, his body relaxed by codeine. I stand by the east window, looking out. The hot noon sun has cut the traffic down; there is a wavy reflection from the tops of parked automobiles. Three or four children walk by, carrying towels rolled around their suits and bathing caps and goggles, on their way to the MDC pool. I hear a siren, rude and insistent, somewhere out of sight.

I cover the remains of his lunch tray with the metal dome and carry it down to the kitchen. As I pass the dining-room door I happen to see his wife at the Victorian sideboard, pouring out a glass of sherry.

They have begun to dig in the street, rerouting the sewer line. A policeman stands in the sun all day, waving traffic out of the way of the feeding steam shovel. The water in the house faucets turns rusty and then dribbles to a stop; the cook goes out to the sidewalk to complain. The men tell her they don't know exactly why the water was cut off, but they connect two hoses to the water pipes in the basement and run them out a window to a metal pipe that links up with the fire hydrant.

Mixed with his annoyance, Charlie is pleased that for the duration he won't have to pay for city water. This seems like a considerable saving to me, since his wife spends something like half the day in the shower. I can hear the water running in the pipes, and sometimes as I'm going up or downstairs with a tray I see her disappearing into her bedroom, her curled hair covered with a plastic shower cap, her robe wrapped tightly around her. It is certainly odd that she stays away from her husband almost completely—too frightened of the cancer to bear becoming involved with it, I suppose.

His secretary telephones from the Cape to announce that she's going to be married. She offers to break in a new girl. He says, "These quacks have put me out of commission for a little while. When you get back from your honeymoon, Grace." He speaks loudly, heartily into the phone. He calls up a jewelry store downtown, managed by a friend of a friend, and has a silverplate coffee service sent to her address. "Wonder what poor sucker she trapped into marriage," he remarks to me with irritation. "Must have got herself pregnant."

The high-pitched buzzing noise of the digging machine seems to intensify his pain. It's harder for him to concentrate on a book or newspaper; he turns the pages absently. His friends, uneasily sensing something malignant, don't stop by to see him so often.

Except for Mick Gowan. He and Charlie have a running joke about a widow Gowan has on the string; she wants to adopt him and set him up on a chicken farm in New Jersey. I keep expecting Gowan to break the news that the pols have dumped him, but he always leaves without saying it.

Charlie asks me to massage his back many times every day. He demands my touch, but is only for the moment comforted by it. I am reminded of a baby rabbit I once saved from the jaws of a cat and put into a box with dandelion leaves and grass. It ate and ate and then suddenly died, and I realized it had been mortally injured after all; the grass spilled out of a gaping hole in its stomach. Charlie's hunger for physical touch is like that, insatiable. And yet I can't fill him.

I notice that he has grown thinner. The ridge of his backbone is accentuated, in spite of the eggs and milk puddings I order from the kitchen. His shoulder blades are sharp under my lubricated palms.

"Why is it that whiskey kills perception of everything else and leaves the pain?" He is restless, leaning on the crutch and superintending the digging, a shot glass in his hand. He turns up the air conditioner. Maybe he has fever, some secondary infection. Or maybe it's just something to do to alter the environment, to compete with the noise of the steam shovel, to exert control.

I shiver and pull on a sweater.

"Are you cold?"

"A little."

I am in a chair; he stands above me. Behind him is the tower of St. John's, inlaid like a mosaic Christmas candy. Our usual roles are reversed. I put off taking the thermometer from its alcohol bath, making the formal notation of his vital signs. There is a faint sweaty smell about him.

"Shall I make tea?"

"You don't like me to drink, do you?"

"Only because it doesn't seem to help a lot."

"Does it frighten you?" I sense that he'd like to be able to frighten me, to have that power. His fingernail touches my ear. "I wouldn't hurt you."

I bob my head out of reach so that my cap is disarranged. "You couldn't hurt me. I have defenses against things like that."

"I don't believe you. You are too young to have a hide that thick." His face is pale; when he leans his head back against the window glass, it shudders in its frame. There is a distortion in the glass—St. John's jumps.

My youth is, I think, something he holds against me. "You're right. I'm always somewhat mixed up. I struggle and struggle against it."

"Maybe you should just give in sometimes," he says gently.

"No, I can't, you know, because of my mother."

"Giving in is not the same thing as caving in."

"That distinction is too tough for me."

"Make some tea, then."

8

The bells in the tower of St. John's strike nine times. In the street the sewer diggers are starting to work, setting yellow cones around the excavation which is still covered with a metal sheet.

Pat's waiting at the trolley stop; he'll be late. He is tall, loose-limbed. His tie, unknotted, hangs around his neck. "How's the old man?" he asks.

"Fine."

"What do you do in there all day—hold his hand?" Gowan must have told him about the fortunetelling. I can just imagine the two of them in the back of the shoe store, gossiping like a pair of biddies.

"Yes." I smile sweetly.

"Are you sore?"

"Here comes your trolley," I say, stepping around a pile of hedge clippings. Mrs. O'Clair has apparently hired someone to attack the front jungle.

When I open Charlie's door, he doesn't turn away from the window. His crutch falls, out of his reach. "You're late. I want you to call Abe Glass for me. I can't get anything out of his answering service. The codeine dose needs to be increased."

"I'm sorry. I happened to meet someone in the street."

"Yes, I saw."

"Just Pat, you know, my landlady's son."

"Is he your boy friend?"

"No. He used to be something like a brother, that's all." I pick up the crutch for him.

"But not now?"

"I hardly see him—I don't know him any more. He just stayed the same after high school, selling shoes. And that's been seven years."

"Whereas *you* are now a woman of the world."

"Don't tease." I hand him the paper cup of tablets and a glass of apple juice. "Do you want to have the dressing changed on the chair or on the bed?"

"I suppose that's one of the tricks they taught you at nursing school." His voice minces, like the Director of Nursing Education: " 'Always give the patient an alternative.' This is a goddamn kindergarten you're running. Apple juice."

"I could quit, you know. What do I care whether you have a clean dressing or not?"

He has lain on the cot; his hands grip the iron head rail. I loosen the tape from his skin, drop the serous, rotten-smelling gauze into a paper bag.

"Don't you care?" he asks at length.

"You do your best to discourage me, it seems." My voice is muffled in the paper mask. I'm glad he can't see the expression on my face; I'd give it all away. With the forceps I pick up the sterile four-by-fours and delicately bury the wound in them. Like snow falling on an ugly piece of landscape: on a factory or strip mine.

He says, "Don't you realize it's because I'm afraid to care about you?"

"Maybe I guessed it, I'm not sure."

"I'm afraid of a lot of things, but that's one of the more pressing. Maureen."

I finish the dressing, wrapping the leg with gauze, and cover his legs with the sheet. I close the books lying by the side of the bed and place them on the table. Morning housekeeping. His silk robe is hung on a hook, his breakfast tray covered, the clock wound. It has begun to rain.

I know that he needs to express anger, but his sucking me into the whirlpool of his emotions makes me feel disconnected. He's edgy, waiting for the codeine to work. Softly I say, "It might be better if Dr. Glass found somebody else."

"You are so damned sensible."

Gran is stretched out on the sofa in the sitting room when I come in from work. Her stockings are rolled down, fat tubes around her ankles. "The ceiling leaked again today. You tell Pat."

"I'll tell him."

"I picked up a few things on sale at Gilchrist's, bargains."

I'm afraid to ask what. The orange fiberglass curtains hanging raggedly behind her were one of her bargains; so was the two-way stretch sofa cover she's lying on. Nothing matches, nothing has any style. I think with a sudden longing of Charlie's white, spare room.

"That's nice." I glance at the front of the evening

newspaper. A fire has gutted three tenements in South Boston: five dead, including a two-month-old infant. Two firemen treated for smoke inhalation at Boston City. There is a photograph of the mother in her bathrobe. The lawn in the background, in clear focus, is covered with debris, but her face is blank, the features indistinct: a trick of the light or of the photographic process. Something about her reminds me of the snapshot in Gran's bureau drawer; my mother was there, sitting on the porch steps, and yet not there. The same is true, I realize, of Uncle Frank's wedding photograph. Only my father is looking into the camera.

"Gran, where did my mother and father live after they were married?"

Gran sits up and ties her shoelaces. "That's a strange question to be asking all of a sudden."

"Where, Gran?"

"They had a place out in Watertown, not too far from your Uncle Frank's. Melendy Avenue, I think it was. Wasn't hardly more than a furnished room." She tucks a slip strap under the sleeve of her housedress. "Of course, it was very hard to find a place then, during the war. They only lived there together a few weeks, while Tim was on furlough. Angie stayed on there after he went overseas, because I had just the one room at the time, over on Pemberton Street, and she wanted to be on her own. Expecting him back and all."

"Why did she leave?"

"Well, I heard about this house, you know—Jack Meaghan's mother was an old friend of mine in the Guild—and Angie and I moved in together. We knew by then your father was missing and she changed her mind about living alone. You were just a few months old. Your bed was right there where the TV is, a big wicker washbasket. That embarrassed Angie, she couldn't afford a bassinet for the public-health nurse to see. I said, the baby don't know the difference. But she just picked on that one thing to be upset about, cried about it for days, I remember."

"Did she talk about my father a lot?"

"No. She just closed her head up tight, wouldn't even listen to talk about him. That's the way she was." Gran takes a barrette out of her stiff yellow-white hair and pins the short wisps tighter. "Angie was so secret, I didn't even know the boy existed, until she told me she was going to marry him. She met him at some dance; he was already a soldier, home on leave."

"Did she love him?"

"She did. Too much."

It is a mixed neighborhood, I can tell from the names on the shops and mailboxes: Armenian, Greek, Italian. The markets are just opening their vegetable stands out on the sidewalks, and in the dusty windows there are rows of glass jars: olives, okra in vinegar, grape leaves. Cloth sacks of rice that one could hardly lift.

On the corner of Melendy Avenue is a down-at-heels gas station, weeds growing in cracks in the asphalt. The street slopes down from the main market street. It looks like rain, and I can feel the dull beginnings of a sore throat when I swallow.

Number 12, where my mother and father lived, is an old three-decker covered with gray asphalt siding. Attached to the front is a row of dilapidated mailboxes, seven of them, of various shapes and periods, the only decoration. The three open porches face the back of the lot. The yard is only plain uncut grass growing behind a wire fence, no flowers or bushes. Next door though, in a vacant lot, there is an enormous weeping-willow tree. It must have been spectacular, even twenty years ago.

In one of the upstairs windows an unshaven man leans against the glass, looking down at me. Because he is the one visible person, and all the other windows have their shades rolled down, I feel it was my mother's room.

I imagine pregnant frightened Angie Mullen sitting there, waiting. Maybe it wasn't so bad for her there if she had that tree to look at. And a baby to feel, growing inside her. She loved him, too much. And then she broke down, became disturbed, got unhinged, went nuts.

I move on, aware of the man's stare. At the lower end of the street is a red brick complex of public-housing units. Around the corner, at the Dexter Spa, I buy a package of peanut-butter crackers and a half-pint carton of milk. All of a sudden I'm ravenous. Then I begin the ride home on the Mt. Auburn Street trolley line.

My raincoat needs waterproofing. I take it to the dry cleaner in Porter Square, which is next to the shoe store where Pat works. The clerk, in a yellow dynel wig—pins for the laundry slips in the corner of her mouth—remarks to the presser, "Full moon tonight, if it don't rain again."

"Ye-as. That's when all the crazies come out."

Monday morning. I'm not wearing my uniform; perhaps I'll stay only long enough to make sure Charlie's all right. My dress is green and white checked gingham, unfashionably long, gathered high above my waist, sleeveless.

He's lying in the rumpled bed. "Jesus, I thought you weren't coming." His blue eyes are extraordinarily pale, as though the pigment is gradually being leached out.

A fork is stuck into the yolk of a fried egg, cold on the plate.

"You haven't eaten your breakfast."

"The grease. I can't stand it."

"Have it boiled, then."

I straighten the sheets, give him the codeine tablets, change the dressing. I lay the back of my hand on his forehead to judge his temperature. It is hot to the touch.

"Maureen, I was terrified you weren't going to come back." He takes my hand and rubs it across his mouth: a rough, hungry sort of kiss. "I need you."

"There's something I must make you understand. I'm really not so strong that you can hang onto me."

"No, don't tell me now." His hands pull me down to the cot.

My eyes are shut; I am at the bottom of something deep and dark.

9

There is a list in the pocket of my sundress: shoe-laces, Butcher's wax, cube-tap, flyswatter, thread. I get off the trolley in front of the florist shop and cross Massachusetts Avenue. Underneath the street at this point is the same spur of the Boston and Maine that passes my house on its way west. Cissy and I used to walk to the shopping center at Porter Square that way, along the tracks, saving the trolley fare to spend on lipstick or chewing gum.

The Saturday-morning crowd, shopping for chicken parts and briquets, is already filling up the parking spaces, though the morning is still cool. I think about how Cissy and I used to go up and down the aisles in Kresge's, choosing what we'd buy if we had the money. What could I get for Charlie that would please him, even if I had a purse bursting with bills?

Kresge's doesn't open until ten. I wait outside in the

Elaine Ford

parking lot. There's the collection box for Morgan Memorial, surrounded by old clothes and shoes spilling out of paper bags. Nobody seems to have been assigned to pick up the castoffs recently; they have an untidy, pawed-over look.

Maybe there are people who come and outfit themselves here at night, trying on things and parading in the parking lot, combining buttonless ruffled blouses with ragged-hemmed skirts. They'd be like the inmates at the mental hospital I used to watch while waiting for Gran to come down from my mother's ward. A whole troop of them, mismatched, limping or straggling, being led out on the lawn for exercise by some poor volunteer. Lipstick ringing mouths like clowns' makeup. Pants dragging: no belts, or they'd hang themselves. One teenaged boy wearing a football helmet, not for the sport but because he was subject to fits.

Kresge's still hasn't opened, though it serves breakfast at the snack bar from eight o'clock on, and there are a few people sitting on the aqua stools. Two middle-aged ladies and I wait inside the door, behind the chain preventing access to the main store.

In the parking lot there is a sudden bone-cracking shriek of brakes; a black limousine and a battered red Volkswagen stop at right angles to each other, inches short of collision. A priest gets out of the black car on the passenger side and strides over to the young mother in the Volkswagen. Her child in the car seat, either frightened or hurt, begins to wail. The priest points his finger, tapping the car window, and shouts at the young woman so that everyone inside Kresge's can hear, "You better watch out, sister!"

The priest, a man maybe sixty with gray hair and a neck sticking out of his clerical collar like a plucked raw turkey, brushes past me into the store and unhooks the chain to let himself through. There is a stunned pause, only a moment; the two ladies and I look at the red Volkswagen, where the child is screaming. Then the car lurches forward, speeding past the Star Market and out of sight. The limousine leaves too, in the other direction.

The priest beckons to one of the salesgirls and has her unlock the cash register at the delicatessen counter. He orders a pound of sliced baked ham, on special sale as advertised, for $1.29. Next to me the ladies mutter to each other, "Did you ever. Him, a priest."

Charlie and I make love to a background of cartoons, turned down to a low pitch, but violent and disconnected. The television set is tuned at random, to disguise all other sounds, but we find this jangling music oddly appropriate. Popeye the Sailor, Felix the Cat. Hip-hip hurray, the mice cry, guns popping, springs sprung.

There are some things undeniably comic about our love-making: the creaking narrow cot, my stubborn virginity, the possibility of his wife's appearing at any moment—though the door is locked. I envision the woman somehow bashing down the door and going at me with a rolling pin.

He tickles my ears and freckled wrists and nipples with his tongue. He convinces me that I am not ugly, after all.

I want to know everything about him, as though by exploring his past I can somehow extend his future. I am less shy of him. He says, "Come to me now, Maureen," and I answer, "No, not yet. Let me inside your head a little bit."

So he tells me about the trip he made to County Cork to discover his roots, about the stone cottage that was his ancestral home and the peat fire that his cousins still keep burning there, about the rain in Dublin alleys and the men he drank with in the public houses by the Liffey.

"But where did you grow up?"

"It's not important. Just a town."

He doesn't really talk about himself; he could just as well have invented those Irish scenes. But I feel myself to be so exposed to him that when he looks at me, he must surely see all the dark and secret pains I've kept hidden up to now. In that way, he's changed me.

I hold his head between my hands, trying to grasp something that I can keep. "Tell me why you love me. Be specific." He smiles, kissing the inside of my wrist. It's almost enough to have him depend on me physically, and yet that very dependence wears me down. His lips on my wrist are rough and cracked.

His face is coarse-grained at such close range. He long ago had acne, often cut himself shaving. There are creases between his eyes, next to his mouth. On his neck are the dead craters of old boils. These defects are both tender and exciting to me. I want to protect him—exactly because he is a man who has always refused protection.

The pain in his leg dwindles. He makes telephone calls, talks about opening the office. The air conditioner is shut off and the casement windows forced open in spite of the heat, for the first time since the house was repainted. We can hear birds nesting in the gutters and also groups of play-schoolers in the street, taken out on expeditions to the firehouse or the park, holding onto lengths of clothes-line for security. A sound truck, announcing a special meeting of the School Committee, circles through the streets: faint, then booming, then faint again. The sewer excavation gradually inches, dug out and then covered over, toward Porter Square.

We lie together on the iron cot, his mouth at my breast. I watch a skywriter spell out over Somerville the letters *l i f e:* the magazine, the cereal, a philosophical question? He sucks, sucks at my breast.

His hand casually strokes my freckled arm. When I give him his tea, I take his hand and fit the cup into it. His need for codeine is less. But he drinks whiskey after I go home; I can tell because in the morning the bottle is emptier.

Some friend of Charlie's is on the telephone. One of his backers in the ward, trying to nose things out. "No, Al, don't bother to come by. I'll tell you, I'm up to my neck in work just now, with Grace gone. Up and married on me, how do you like that? I'll see you at Rotary. Save me a place."

On trash collection days there are cardboard boxes full of odds and ends on the sidewalk in front of the O'Clair house: shrunk sweaters, photograph albums, canceled checks, dented saucepans. An orderly person, his wife.

When I collect my check at the end of the two-week period she looks up from her desk and asks, "How is . . . my husband?" Bitterly, I think that if she'd ever bother to go up there she might find out for herself. But I'm just as glad she doesn't.

"He seems better," I answer noncommittally.

She nods and picks up her crochet square. She's got her television set tuned in to a rerun of *Leave It to Beaver.* Time can be controlled that way, I suppose, rows of crochet matched to quarter-hour sections of situation comedy. I pity her. How old she looks. There is an empty sherry glass on the windowsill.

"Would you like to sit down?"

"Oh, I'm afraid I can't," I say, folding the check and putting it in my uniform pocket. "I have to cook supper for my grandmother."

"I expect he'll recover in time for the campaign."

I look at her in disbelief. Witless woman. Doesn't she realize he's going to die?

"Well, time will tell," she says complacently. The pity drains out of me. I turn and go down the stairs.

The lesion on his leg has opened up again; the tissue around it is breaking down. Metastasis in the calf, I guess. The bloody drainage is bright red. Dr. Glass stops around more often on his way home from hospital rounds, and sometimes he does the dressing change for me, though he's more awkward at it. It's puzzling: I've seen those big brown hands tie the tiniest of surgical knots in the operating room, but with the powdery gloves off he seems to mislay his experienced grace.

The wound is ugly, but it's my connection to Charlie. Somehow it's mixed up in my mind with his penetration of me, also bloody, and his deft exploration of my body. As Dr. Glass fumbles with disposable plastic forceps I glance out the window and see a pair of nuns shuffle along the sidewalk, maybe on their way to Confession.

I hear Charlie say, "It's getting worse, isn't it, Abe?" and I am curiously exhilarated, as though he's said, "I'm getting in deeper with her."

But Dr. Glass only says, "It's hot as hell in here. The air conditioner gone on the fritz?" and goes to scrub his hands in the bathroom, leaving the remains of the sterile pack for me to dispose of.

In the back of my mind the priest is shouting, "You better watch out, sister."

10

Cissy comes up the back stairs after supper and sits at the kitchen table between Gran and me, like she always used to. The three of us have a cup of tea together. Cissy takes a pack of cigarettes out of her handbag—she's taken up smoking since I've seen her last—and uses her saucer for an ashtray. "I can only stay a minute, because Vince is taking care of Ronny while I do the shopping. He gets awful mean if I leave him with the kid too long."

Gran puts an extra spoonful of sugar into her tea; she knows I won't say anything with Cissy there. "I've missed you, Cissy. Maureen hardly sees a soul these days."

"Well, I know she's busy with her job, and the kid sure keeps me hopping. I get so nervous I don't gain an ounce." She pauses to let the implication settle in and fiddles with her cigarette. "Even though I'm expecting again."

"Cissy, that's great. When?"

"New Year's. Vince is counting on it to be the first baby of the year and win us a washing machine. But I hope I don't get my picture in the paper. I looked awful when Ronny was born."

Cissy knows she looked fine, with her cute nose everyone says is just like Doris Day's and her frosted bouffant hair-do. She made a point, I remember, of going home from the hospital in a knitted suit, and the baby was dressed in a miniature football outfit.

"Anyway, Maurey, I was thinking about your birthday coming up this week and how we always used to do something together on our birthdays. Like remember the time we went to see *Gone with the Wind* downtown and had banana splits afterward and got lost?"

"And we both had terrible blisters on our feet because we wore our Sunday shoes without socks to look grownup, and we had to walk and walk to find the MTA entrance."

Cissy giggles. "We were too embarrassed to ask anybody. I was so hot and stuffed with banana split I thought I was going to faint. Still, we had to buck up, just like Scarlett." She sighs, as though that was the best day of her life. She notices that her cigarette has soaked up the slopped-over tea in her saucer and gone out.

"Well, what I came over for was, I thought maybe you could come to our place for dinner on Friday. Would you mind, Gran?"

"Course not. Do her good to get out."

"Well, Vince's ice cream is out there melting." At the door Cissy stops, fumbling for the car keys in her plastic handbag. "How is Charlie O'Clair, anyway? Somebody told me he's in a pretty bad way. It must be depressing, working there."

I wonder what kind of question this is, because Cissy is looking down, tossing it off. "No, it's not so bad. I've seen a lot worse."

Cissy has been my best friend since kindergarten, when the Fairlies moved into the ramshackle brown house around the corner on Middlesex Street. Cissy had seven brothers and sisters, all older. Her big sister Irene wet the bed, the reason I wasn't allowed upstairs, I guess—or maybe there was some even more sinister reason. Irene is now a nun, Sister Mary Teresa. One brother was killed in Korea. Her sister-in-law Margie used to nurse her baby, leaning against the icebox in the Fairlies' kitchen; it was the first time I ever saw a woman's breast. There was always dog hair in the rug, football helmets in the breakfast nook, Elvis on the radio.

The Fairlies had a swing in their back yard, hanging on ropes from an oak tree so big that nothing else would ever grow in the yard. On summer afternoons Cissy and I sat together on the swing and twisted the ropes around and around and then let go and whirled the reverse way until we were dizzy and nauseated. But because we had nothing else to do, in a little while we'd start the ropes creaking around again. I could smell Cissy's decaying baby teeth, sitting so close to her. The police dog, tied up because it bit, would strain on its leash and reach its tongue under the dripping outside faucet.

We made our First Communion together, wearing identical white net dresses, but different sizes, because I was taller. Cissy was given a gold cross on a chain by her godmother, and then she lost it in our secret place in the lilac bushes next to my house. It's probably still there, hidden somewhere in the thicket. She cried for days over it, but the ceremony itself, eating Christ's body, did not seem to touch her, as it did me.

In the summer dusk Mrs. Fairlie leaned out of an upstairs window and called "Ca-ceel-ya," and that meant the end of hide-and-go-seek for both of us, because somehow Mrs. Fairlie had more authority than Gran. Even though Gran looked down on Mrs. Fairlie because of her big disorderly family crammed into that broken-down house. The two ladies had different canasta sets, and the Fairlies came from Somerville.

Once in a while Cissy left for home in a hurry, looking stricken, because she had a terrible toothache, but then she'd be back in a little while, smelling powerfully of oil of cloves.

It was from Cissy that I first heard about menstruation, and later received a whispered, somewhat confused description of the sex act. The impression I got was that intercourse was supposed to be accomplished sitting up, face to face; I had a hard time imagining the logistics of it. The whole thing depressed me, since I've always been clumsy at gymnastics. It would probably be easier not to get married at all.

In high school we did our homework together, sitting at Gran's kitchen table and listening to the top forty hits on the radio. But in the winter of our senior year, Cissy began to fix herself up a little better and was taken up as a kind of mascot by some members of the Girls' Athletic Club, to which she was elected. She developed a gift for sharp little wisecracks. After a few months she began to go steady with a second-string football player, wearing his class ring on a chain around her neck, and she bleached a streak in her hair. She spelled her nickname with an *i* at the end and dotted it with a circle. When I was filling out applications to nursing schools, Cissy was cutting articles out of *Bride* magazine.

After Cissy's wedding that summer, all the cars leaving the church trailed crepe-paper streamers and sounded their horns, just as they did after a winning football game. "Mrs. Vincent Ranelli" on her pale-pink stationery.

Charlie is asking for milk in his tea now; the lemon tastes too sour. "The sore isn't going to heal, is it? You can see practically down to the bone. I pretend not to look when you change the bandage, but I see it."

"No, it's going to be all right."

He doesn't answer; his hand grasps my neck. Our love-making is both mechanical and frantic now. He's hardly up to it. The cartoons on Channel 14 from Worcester are accompanied by piano-roll ragtime and the flat characters, dancing, are closely accompanied by ghosts.

Cissy's face is blotchy; she's had a hard day, she tells me. She leans back on her heels, beginning to show her pregnancy, and the child Ronny pulls at her legs, whining to be picked up. The apartment smells of his diapers—or of boiled broccoli, I'm not sure which—and of sour milk. There's an untidy, distracted air to the place, the area rug slipping out of position, the exhaust fan refusing to operate. Some minor scuffle explodes down on Inman Street and a bottle splinters against a stop sign.

I sit in a kitchen chair while Cissy skins the hot potatoes and then mashes them. This situation is awkward, unaccustomed; we both assume guest-host manners. I admire her curtains, which are figured with alternating orange coffee grinders and gold potbellied stoves.

"I don't know why Vince isn't home, I told him you were coming. The shift ends at five-thirty." She swings Ronny onto her hip and picks up her dying cigarette out of the ashtray.

"It's all right, Cissy, really. I'm not hungry yet."

"You eat with Charlie O'Clair?"

"He has a cook. She fixes two trays."

"What about his wife?"

"She doesn't take the time. She's out a lot, playing bridge or something. It's a big house to run."

"But only the two of them there."

"Well, she gardens. Besides, she's a little confused."

"I'll say. Remember we used to see her buying candy, right up at the counter with all the little kids. Imagine that old crow stuffing herself with chocolate babies and jelly beans. Gives me the creeps."

"I'd forgotten that."

She looks at me curiously. "Why do you suppose he married her, anyway? He's quite a looker. I heard he was going to run for City Council now that Kelly's retiring, but then he got the cancer. Is he going to get over it?"

"Perhaps."

"You don't say much."

"I know, Cissy. I can't."

She looks flattened. She's had no career, no need for professional ethics. I guess she thought she one-upped me by marrying first, but now it dawns on her that maybe she was a little hasty. Just diapers and bottles all day long, no interesting secrets any more.

She settles Ronny in his high chair. "I hope the new baby's a girl. I love those little dresses with lace and all. Oh hell, why don't we eat? Vince is probably in some bar."

Ronny bangs on his high-chair tray with a plastic rabbit that looks like a relic from last year's Easter basket.

"Believe me, I'm hungry all the time." Cissy cuts the pork roast into thick, fat-laden slices. "Oh ... music." The food grows cold on the dinette table while Cissy sorts through the albums. Ronny leans over his tray and drops the rabbit to the floor, grunting at me to retrieve it for him. Then the record starts.

"*Candlelight Duet.* I gave it to Vince last Christmas."

"It's romantic."

Cissy's mouth is pinched with nervous hospitality, and her honesty is a kind of reflex. "He hardly ever plays it though."

We begin to eat, delicately cutting the fat and bone away from the meat. Cissy's talking about our old history teacher from sophomore year; she'd run into her the week before when she was cashing Vince's pay check at the bank. "I had Ronny with me, in his stroller. It was crazy, I felt all of a sudden older than her, because she never had babies, you know."

"Maybe she didn't want them."

"Oh no, nobody ever asked her, that's all. Speaking of which, what about you?"

"Nobody's asked me, either."

"No, you don't get my point. Vince has a friend at the plant, a real nice guy. We could fix you up."

"Thanks, I'm not up to blind dates now. I *am* kind of depressed, I guess."

The door bangs, and Vince drops his jacket on a chair. He's a stocky man with black sideburns and a roll of beer-fed fat above his belt. "What's for dinner?"

"You're late." Cissy pulls Ronny out of his high chair and hitches up his rubber pants. She holds the struggling child away from her distended abdomen.

"I had to do overtime. Two of the men were out on my shift."

"It's Maureen's birthday."

"You don't have to dive right into the food."

"You could've called."

"I could've, but the work had to be done first. Then I thought it would be quicker just to come on home. Happy birthday, Maureen."

"Why can't somebody else do the work, just for once, when those deadbeats decide they're not going to show up?"

"Cissy. When the promotion to foreman comes up, I'd like to be the one they pick to do the job. If you don't mind. Ah, the hell with it." He sits at the table with his can of beer and stabs a slice of pork on the platter. "Where'd you get this stuff? All fat, hardly any meat to it."

"As you know very well, I don't have all that much money to spend for prime cuts." She carries Ronny off to his room. The record comes to an end and is discarded by the hi-fi machine. In the silence Vince and I can hear a diaper being rinsed in the flushing toilet.

He opens a second beer and pours some into my glass. "She's dumb, Cissy is. She really has a very small mind."

"She's tired."

"Well, take you. You're a working girl and you don't all crumple up all the time."

"How do you know?"

"I can tell, that's all." His hand comes down on my arm, his fingers twiddle on my skin. Stories go around about nurses. "We should see more of you around here. Maybe you could teach her a lesson or two."

Cissy is pouring milk into a plastic nursing bottle in the kitchen. She screws the nipple on while Ronny whines in his crib. Two flies circle under the overhead light.

Vince pushes his plate to the center of the table, unbuckles his belt and lets it out a notch. The black hair on his belly curves around his navel. "Well, she's good for some things, anyway," he says, tucking the shirt in and going to the other end of the room to turn the knob on the television set.

The offhand pass—if that's what it was—makes me feel unclean. I don't think he would have done it when I was still a virgin. Can people really tell, just by looking at me?

I long to be with Charlie, to be reassured that I am loved.

I scrape the dishes into the garbage pail and stack them by the sink. "Cissy, I really should go. I promised to have some birthday cake with Gran."

"Oh. I understand."

"But it was great to see you."

"Just like old times."

"Sure."

"Vince would be glad to drive you home."

"No—thanks anyway. I have an errand to do on the way."

I am opening the door at the bottom of the stairs before Cissy calls to me. "Your birthday present. I forgot to give it to you." I go back halfway; we meet in the dark stairwell. Our faces are close together as Cissy puts the holiday-wrapped package in my hand.

"Maureen. You're lucky, you know." This is the closest we've come in years to returning to our childhood intimacy.

"You'll be okay, Cissy." I'm saying things like this all the time and my voice sounds false in my own ears. I just don't want to hear about her troubles.

On the way home I unwrap the package. It's a pair of bandage scissors, not such good quality as the pair I already own, but I'm sure it wasn't easy for her to find the money for it. I get off the trolley at the stop across from Charlie's house, thinking I'll go in to see him just for a moment. His wife would have to let me in, though; the kitchen door would be locked at this time of night. I picture the woman at the door, her mouth crammed with chocolate babies. I just walk on home.

11

Charlie sets up his chessboard to study a problem from the Sunday newspaper. "The Panov Attack in the Caro-Kann Defense," he says. "Knight takes pawn transposes to a position of the Queen's Gambit accepted." His concentration, the sound of pieces being moved on the board, excite me. He rubs the pawn between thumb and forefinger.

"Maybe you could teach me the moves."

"Yes ... sometime." He's drowsy; he's already lost interest in the problem.

"I don't understand it, Maureen. There's pain in the good leg."

"Have you mentioned it to Dr. Glass?"

"I guess it's my imagination."

He presses his head to my belly, as though listening. He no longer makes love to me; the balance has tipped, and the need for codeine is more imperative than his sexual longings. There are swellings in his groin.

When Dr. Glass comes in he glances at the chess-board, picks up a black bishop and moves it experimentally to several alternative positions. "I think what you've got is a little phlebitis in the left leg. We'll have Maureen put some hot packs on it, see if that doesn't help."

"Why doesn't the sore on the other leg heal?"

"Give it time. You young men are so impatient."

"My practice is going to wrack and ruin. Not to mention plans for the campaign."

"You can pick it all up again easy enough."

"Can I, Abe?"

"What are you asking me?"

"Nothing."

The chess pieces on the board make me think of tombstones: reminders of death inhabiting everything.

"Maureen, am I going to die?"

"No." I check the heat on his leg, unwrapping the plastic covering. I soak the flannel in hot water and wring it out before laying it back along his thigh and tucking the towel around it.

"Why does it hurt so much?"

"I don't know. Things like that are mysterious sometimes."

"I see, you think the pain is some defect in my soul."

"I don't believe your soul has any defects." He kisses me, pulling my hair between his fingers.

I count his pulse and at the same time listen to his wind-up clock ticking. I wrap the blood-pressure cuff around his arm and pump it up, but when I put the plugs of the stethoscope in my ears, it's my own heart I feel beating.

Dr. Glass knocks out his pipe into the brass ashtray on the front hall table. I touch his sleeve.

68

"The hot packs don't seem to be doing much for the pain."

"No, I'm afraid not. It's all mumbo-jumbo, Maureen."

"What do you mean?"

"There's no phlebitis. But I have to let him think I'm doing *something*."

"The cancer has metastasized to the other leg, then."

His mouth opens in a grimace, baring gold-tipped teeth. "Good God, Maureen, it's all over the place."

I pass his wife on the stair. The woman seems to me like a person whose mind races crazily behind a frozen face. She wears unpleasantly heavy perfume on her bird-like body.

The August weather is dry. I find Charlie looking out the raised bathroom window. On the lawn a flock of large gray birds are pecking up seed. He's been having trouble urinating; he struggles back and forth to the bathroom on his crutch, not wanting to admit it to me.

"Why am I so weak? I've never been like this before."

I stand next to him and put my arm around his waist. He grips my wrist with bony, blue-veined fingers. "I'm not an old man."

"I know."

He laughs bitterly. "I've even tried praying. But I've come to the conclusion that no one is listening."

When I think of prayer, I see Gran's black-beaded rosary in the top drawer of her bureau, tangled in an old hairnet. "I want to believe, I long to. I was always thought to be very devout. At one time they thought I was going to become a nun, but I was play-acting most of the time. Even my grandmother, who is pretty much of an old faker herself, never suspected."

"Why did you want to fool them?"
"Oh, it was myself I was trying to fool."

"Am I going to die, Maureen?"
"Yes."

12

When I'm walking by the shoe store on my way to pick up my raincoat at the dry cleaner, Gowan sees me from the window. His face is full of smiles—wrinkled as a week-old balloon, though he can't be any older than Charlie.

"Come in a minute, Maureen."

A sale's going on. Rubber flip-flops from Japan, open-toed wedgies, mules and scuffs, all tangled together in a great bin. Pat's at the other end of the store, waiting on a couple of girls. He doesn't notice me.

"There's a letter in the mail, Maureen." Gowan is serious now.

"To me?"

"To Charlie. He'll probably get it Monday morning."

"About the Council race?"

"They're going with Gallagher this time."

"I suppose you enjoyed giving them the inside dope."

His look of surprise is pained, but maybe it's just good acting. "I didn't say anything. Everybody seemed to know."

"All right, skip it."

"Maybe you could say something to him to prepare him, before he opens the letter."

"It doesn't matter any more, Gowan. He knows he's dying."

He's silent for a moment. "I'll get you some coffee."

I sit in a corner and pick up a foot measure, slide the metal indicator back and forth. Pat's very busy with the two girls. His smooth blond hair slips over his eyes when he kneels. He tosses it back, returning boxes of rejects to the shelves. Then he sees me and gives me a wave. He's handsome. No single feature particularly outsized, unusual, distorted. No pimples or scars. He does everything easily and without thought: pushing the shoeboxes into their proper cubbyholes, flipping a shoe over in his hand to note the size stamped underneath, bending heel to toe a couple of times to give it flexibility.

One of the girls is wearing a sleeveless jersey; she shivers in the air conditioning. She has red hair and puffy, lashless eyelids. Her legs are bare.

The girl friend nudges her. "Those are kinda chintzy for eight ninety-five. Look the way the bow is stapled on crooked."

"Who's buying, her or you?" Pat's voice is so polite it's almost an invitation.

"Well, I might get a pair, if I see something I like." The girl friend has piano legs and a bosom that seems to be contained in some kind of harness; I can see the outlines under her shirt. Her legs have plenty of dark stubbly hair.

Pat takes a pair of sandals out of tissue paper. They have long leather straps and a fresh, raw smell. "Just came in this morning." Pat laces the narrow straps around the redhead's legs, all the way up to her knees. Both girls are leaning over to watch, breathing audibly.

"Groovy," the girl friend whispers.

While the redhead's admiring her feet in the mirror, Pat brings another pair for the girl friend. Slowly he laces up the straps.

Gowan sighs, handing me a container of coffee. "Not even out of the sale bin. I wish I had his touch."

The medication has been switched to meperidine, by injection. I thrust the needle into the vial and pull back on the syringe so that it fills with the drug. I caress the muscle in his thigh to make it relax before jabbing the needle in.

"I'm not an old man, Maureen."

I snap the needle in its plastic cap off the end of the syringe, drop the two halves into the wastebasket.

"I know you aren't."

"Does it seem fair? Just speaking objectively, now, on a scale of one to ten. Do I deserve it less or more than most?"

"Don't torture me with questions like that." I go to the bathroom and look at my face in the mirror. There is a white circle around my mouth. I turn the fat porcelain faucet hard to make it stop its slow drip and then go back and lay my hand on his back.

"No. I didn't mean that. You have to talk about it."

"When my wife comes up here she's hardly in the door before she's complaining about the tax bill, the kids messing around in the playhouse, the cook embezzling grocery money, or some damn silly thing."

"She's frightened."

"Aren't you, then?"

"Yes, but I've had more experience, maybe. And she's your wife, after all. She had your child."

"What do you know about that?"

"Oh, you know, you hear things."

"My child is dead."

The drug warms his extremities, mutes his brain. He turns his cheek to the pillow and sleeps. I stand by the window and watch the cars go by, the trolleys at five-minute intervals, old ladies on their way to church. My nerves are just about shot. I peel the skin from my lower lip with my fingernail until I can taste the salt and rust flavor of my own blood.

As I'm leaving the house in the early evening, pulling on my raincoat, Mrs. O'Clair appears in the doorway of the drawing room. She's wearing a buttoned-up cardigan; the little tucked lines around her mouth are working.

"My husband knows he's going to die, doesn't he? You told him."

"Yes."

She puts the sherry glass to her lips with care, so as not to spill the drink. The liver marks on her hands seem darker.

"You may not believe it, but he is not a strong man. You would call it sensitive, I suppose; I know better. It was foolish to tell him."

"There's a point where people have to come to terms with dying; there's no use hoping it will go away."

"If only he can, Miss Mullen."

"It's more cruel not to be truthful."

"He makes his own truth. Oh yes, I know him very well."

This is not very perceptive, I think. I make a move toward the kitchen, to leave by the back door. But the woman picks at the buttons on her sweater and pulls me back with her prying, wheedling voice. "Wait, please wait." Her hair is perfectly arranged, her collar bleached white and edged with minute webs of lace. "I wonder if you could give me some idea of how much time he has left. There are so many things to arrange . . ." She closes her eyes, squeezing tears from them.

"No. I don't know at all."

"You see, his law practice—I'll have to find some-body . . ." So that's what she is thinking of, the stability of her income. She has to find some lawyer to buy the practice, if that's how those things are managed, without Charlie guessing what she's up to.

"You'd better ask Dr. Glass."

"Yes, of course." She is swaying delicately against the door frame, her eyes half shut. Probably been sipping sherry since breakfast.

"I'm sorry, my grandmother's waiting for me."

What would happen if I left this house and never came back?

The windows are closed, the air conditioner again in operation.

Charlie has been dreaming. "I am in a warm salty sea. There doesn't seem to be any question of drown-ing—the water is so buoyant I don't even have to swim—but I am drifting, bobbing along, farther and farther from shore. The odd thing is, I don't seem to mind. I turn my head, expecting to see you there on the edge of the sand, but the shore has changed and turned into a rocky vol-canic island, deserted except for a bunch of birds, which fly suddenly into the air, screaming to each other. The way seagulls do over orange peels in the water."

"It sounds like a movie."

"Much more real than that. I can still feel the water rippling on my skin."

*　　*　　*

"Will you have tea?"

"It doesn't taste good to me any more. I don't know why." He's eating soda crackers to minimize his nausea. We still tune in to the cartoons on Channel 14, enjoying the violent craziness. He drifts in and out of sleep.

Dr. Glass talks to me in the hall. "We're going to have to move him back to the hospital soon. He's getting dehydrated, no doubt the fluid and electrolyte balance out of whack."

"No, not yet. I'll get him to drink more, some way."

"Here's the house key, then. You can let yourself in whenever you like."

"Won't his wife mind?"

"No, why should she?"

I shrug.

"Do you sleep at night, Maureen?"

"The nausea is catching, I guess."

"You must drink something, Charlie."

"No, not tea. The taste is so bitter."

"Water, then. Or juice. I want you to stay here with me."

"Do you care that much about me, Maureen?"

"Why do you keep asking?"

"Everything is misty, dissolving. Even the pain goes away. I'm losing myself." He drinks water, to please me, as though it is medicine. The mail brings comic greeting cards, exhorting him to health. Sometimes the names they are signed with escape him; he imagines they were delivered by mistake. "Probably some client I've forgotten." He moves restlessly in the bed, picking at the sheet.

I go to the bathroom and vomit, quietly, so he can't hear.

13

Gowan's face peeps out from behind a great bunch of snapdragons. "I'm just leaving these for Charlie. Don't wake him."

"He'll be pleased."

"You look worn out, Maureen."

"I'm all right."

"Really?"

"Sure."

Some of the snapdragon blossoms have fallen to the carpet in the upstairs hall. They look like popcorn. I start to pick them up and Gowan says, above my head, "I have a cottage on the beach. It belongs to my aunt, actually. But she's too old to go there any more and I thought—I've been thinking I could take you there for a weekend. Like they say, a change is as good as a rest. I'd even do the cooking."

His invitation is so unexpected that I almost laugh.

"I'm a good cook."

"I'm sure you are."

"Will you think about it?"

"Won't your widow mind?"

"That's Charlie's joke. Not mine." He's so kind, it's impossible to refuse without hurting him.

"Yes, I'll think about it."

Crickets are courting in the bushes; it's the first time I've noticed them this year. I let myself in the kitchen door with Dr. Glass's key and go upstairs.

Charlie doesn't look surprised to see me back again after supper; perhaps he's losing the sense of time being parceled into ordinary segments. I sit on the edge of the cot but don't touch him.

After he drinks, he says, "I was lonely."

"Just now?" But he's not thinking of me.

"She was pretty and pliant, her hair was like silk then." His eyes close and I think he's fallen asleep, but then his breath catches. "When the baby was born, I found out how cruel and selfish she is. I could never feel the same way about her after that." His grip on my wrist is surprisingly strong. "Do you understand, Maureen?"

"I think so."

He opens my hand and sees the key.

"It's yours," I say.

"Why do you hold it like that?"

"It's solid. Look what happens when I close my fist around it tight enough." The imprint of the key is in my palm, even the sawtoothed edge. He once saw good luck there.

"And I myself am slipping away."

"Not yet, Charlie."

"You made a mistake—the key isn't really mine."

He struggles out of the cot, limping on his crutch,

and finds something under a pile of handkerchiefs in his bureau—an old-fashioned pocket watch. "It was my grandfather's. He was nearly blind by the time I knew him, but he could still do magic tricks, extracting the watch from behind my ear." He winds it and sets it according to the bedside clock, then pulls a knob and the watch sounds nine miniature chimes. "And he could always tell the time. To the nearest hour anyway, he said that would do." He snaps the watch face shut and puts it in my hand. "You like old things."

"Yes."

"It's all I have to give you, Maureen. All the rest is hers."

Holding the watch, I wonder why he denies possessing the house or anything in it. Perhaps it is the revulsion to dying here.

I meet Gowan in Porter Square after work on Friday and we take the trolley and subway to South Station, where we catch the commuter bus to Marshfield. We have to stand, hanging onto metal bars and each other for support. The bus is full of exhaust fumes and cigarette smoke; I feel dizzy and lightheaded. I wish I'd thought to bring some crackers in my suitcase.

The bus creeps along the Southeast Expressway, trapped in the rush-hour traffic, over Dorchester, past the gas tanks and Neponset Circle. Gowan's next to me. The coarse material of his tweed jacket touches my skin. Too hot for summer, too big for him. We don't try to make conversation. I wonder whether he wants my body. I don't feel anything at all about him.

The traffic thins south of Quincy, in the area of spare pine woods and grassy fields. The packed, illuminated bus picks up speed. We seem to be hurtling forward, through the calm jigsaw of marshes, on some wild human juggernaut.

We get off the bus on Ocean Street and decide to have some coffee at the lunch counter in the bakery before beginning the walk up Winslow. He's long over his cup, though the counter girl is anxious to close and is pulling the shades in the windows and unplugging the Silex. Perhaps he's worried about what he's got himself into. I notice that one of his cuff buttons is hanging by only a thread and offer to sew it on for him. He tugs the button off and puts it in his pocket. "Never mind."

The cottage is two blocks inland from the ocean, overlooking the marsh, where the sun sets. He shows me my room. "We'll have a swim when you're ready." The room had once been a laundry room; a shorted-out washer-dryer combination is in the corner, next to a folded-up aluminum cot. All around the washing machine the asphalt tile flooring is peeling. There's no closet. I hang my dress on a wire hanger from the curtain rod and change into my bathing suit. It's a yellow halter-neck, not flattering, I know, but the only one I have. Gran found it at some sale.

The tide is high. Gowan and I walk down to the ocean, picking up our tender city feet over pebbles and bits of washed-up straw. Everyone else on the beach is brown and supine in the fading light; Gowan and I look more naked for being white. His body is even thinner than I'd thought.

We wade in together, the icy tide bubbling around our ankles like soapsuds, but then we swim separately, without communicating. Gowan leaves the water first, finding his towel on the high-water line. I tread water for a while, watching the seagulls circle over the jetty. Then I walk back to the cottage alone.

Surprise. Pat's in the kitchen drinking a beer and Gowan's at the stove frying up a batch of clams.

"We've got a party now," Gowan says.

"How did you get here? There's only one bus."

Pat grins. "My mother's car. Didn't you see it outside?"

"No."

"Brain full of cobwebs." Gowan lifts the wire basket out of the sizzling fat and dumps a pile of clams on a platter. "Hurry and get dressed. Wait till you taste these, Maureen. I should have been a cook."

"I thought it was a safecracker you should have been."

"Anything's better than selling shoes—right, Pat?"

"The world sure has a lot of feet in it." Pat pours me a beer. Their gaiety is catching; I laugh more than I have in a long time.

After supper we build a fire out of driftwood and chunks of cannel coal, and the three of us sit on the rug drinking beer. Sea salt on the wood snaps. Gowan sings: "She drives a wheelbarrow through streets wide and narrow, crying cockles and mussels, alive, alive-o.

> *"Alive, alive-o*
> *Alive, alive-o*
> *Crying cockles and mussels*
> *Alive, alive-o."*

Later, lying in bed, I can hear motorcycles racing on the road and, much more indistinctly, the sound of the tide draining away from the beach. I realize I have been asleep. Pat and Gowan are still up talking; they must have gone through the whole case of beer.

I hear Pat say, "This will make you laugh, Gowan. I always loved her, I always did. She was too young."

* * *

I am distressed to find how much Charlie has failed by Monday morning. There is a yellow cast to his face; the cancer has hit the liver. Over the weekend Dr. Glass hired two more shifts of nurses to maintain around-the-clock care. The wound is enlarged, suppurating, surrounded by a sinister area of purple flesh, but the wet packs have been abandoned.

There is a new sharing of the mystery that makes treatment more efficient but cuts between Charlie's and my special understanding. He's reaching out to the others now, even his wife. She has begun to read Dickens to him in the afternoons, sitting in the chair by the north window. Joe Gargery threatening Pip: "I'll have your heart and liver out," in her flat, wheedling voice. She wears a linen suit and a ruffled blouse; on her lapel is the egg-shaped pin encrusted with tiny jewels.

Father Smythe, a priest who was a classmate of Pat's at high school, insinuates himself into the circle with his rubbery grin and black prayerbook and, to my surprise, is not sent away.

Going to the South Shore has rearranged everything. He's lost to me now.

14

The child, though only a raspberry-sized cluster of cells, seems to fill my whole belly. I crave to feed it with milk and pastries, protect it with fat. In some way that I would find hard to describe, my own existence depends on the well-being of the child.

I stand in the hall, looking into his wife's bedroom. There is a four-poster bed covered with a net canopy, starched curtains in the window, pale-green wall-to-wall carpeting. She is upstairs, with him.

Maybe the hope is that wall-to-wall insulates you from things like death, but it won't work; probably in the end she is more vulnerable, more apt to lose her bearings. I have become aware of a steady inner core in my own body. I'm almost frightened by the power, but with the flick of an eyelid I could imagine away Charlie O'Clair, our interdependence, this convoluted house. The only real things now are myself and the replication of self.

* * *

"The sky is falling, Chicken Little."

It looks that way; a swirl of green leaves, prematurely torn from their branches, slap against the windows. Nearly Labor Day. The storm, as though heralding the end of summer, brings a drop in temperature.

The ambulance arrives at the door, also a police car; the officer is an old friend of Charlie's. I've already packed his toilet articles and dressing gown. The ambulance attendants strap him to the stretcher; the police officer escorts his wife, who will accompany him in the ambulance, along with the night-shift nurse. Father Smythe is there, smiling his boyish, eye-squeezing smile. Charlie doesn't look back at me or even at the room. He's exchanging weak jokes with the ambulance attendants as they carry him down the stairs.

I am the only one left in the room. After the ambulance pulls away from the curb, lights flashing, I strip the cot, count the codeine tablets and syringes, unplug the hotplate, television set and air conditioner, pack the chess pieces in their box. The last thing he said to me: the sky is falling. Not such a joke. He ended up by resenting me— after everything—my youth and health. I watch the raindrops, enormous crystal ones, begin to collide with the slate roof.

I've always hated last times: the last Latin class, though Latin tortured me, the last time Cissy and I went shopping together before she married, though by then we had little enough to say to each other. I rinse out the teapot and leave it in its usual place on the windowsill, and then place the house key next to it.

As I shut the front door behind me, a trolley wheezes up to the stop in front of the house. Two old ladies, signaling imperiously with their umbrellas, are waiting to

board. On impulse I jump on behind them. I open my
purse for change, leaning against the vertical bar as the
trolley lurches forward, and am surprised to find that my
hand is shaking, not quite under my control. Several pennies and dimes bounce on the floor and roll down the
steps. I slide into a seat, though from the looks on the
faces of the other riders, I gather that I'm expected to do a
balancing act on the steps and pick up all those coins.
Young people don't know the meaning of money.

The trolley hisses and jerks past Porter Square and
on toward Harvard; the driver curses the traffic. A little
rain clogs everything up. We careen into the tunnel under
Harvard Square and stop. End of the run, no ceremony.
The door opens on a dark wall; unless you push your way
to the back, you have to cross in front of the trolley to get
to the subway or the street. I always half expect that the
driver's going to start off before I get across; it's something like Russian roulette, though I've never read in the
paper about anyone getting maimed that way. It is dank
even in the tunnel, rain dripping in somewhere and
tracked in on people's feet.

For a moment I consider going up the escalator, then
remember the rain and wind, and push instead through
the turnstile to the subway. The platform is emptier than
I'm used to seeing it, the commuters all at work, the gap
between summer and regular university students not yet
filled, the suburban matrons already plowing the aisles in
Filene's basement or else put off by the storm.

A giant billboard on the opposite side of the tracks
advertises a funeral home: for Peace of Mind when it
Matters Most.

The Ashmont subway is comforting, anonymous; I
like sitting on the bench and staring at the passengers
across from me, imagining things about their lives. Of

course, I myself am invisible. Harvard, Central, Kendall, Charles, Park, Washington: the order of stations goes through my mind like an incantation or litany. The journey's dividend is when the train suddenly hits the light of day as the railway bridge rises over the Charles, and there is the pewter-gray city shrouded in mist. A mysterious civilization emerging out of the ground—though nobody else ever looks very surprised. And then the train digs under again.

I get off at Washington Street, along with the last trickle of bargain hunters, who hold their handbags against their bosoms like shields. Someone ahead of me hurries up the steps in a red rubber raincoat. She might be Cissy; the two of us are twelve, going to eat hotdogs at the Sunspot and try on Shetland sweaters in Filene's. The great sin of our childhoods, eating hotdogs on Friday. But the girl clutches her mother to turn into Jordan's basement, and I can see that her hair is black and her face dotted with moles, nothing like Cissy.

Another level upstairs, to the street. At that moment a newspaper is lifted off the stack at the newsdealer's; by a trick of wind the sheets separate and wrap around me, as though I am being gift-wrapped, or mummified.

The old crab of a man yells after me, "Hey, you didn't pay!"

In one of the office buildings I order a cup of hot chocolate, standing at the carry-out counter in the cafeteria. There's a strange muted buzzing in my ears, as though they've been plugged with something, or partly deadened with novocain. The waitress says something to me, leaning across the jelly rolls. "Abbie."

"What?"

"Hurricane Abbie. Four inches of rain before rush hour."

She drops my mug into the dishpan. "You'll want to get where you're going, won't you, dear?"

The rain has stopped for the moment, but it's so dark outside the streetlights flicker. Farther down Washington Street I see on a marquee: *Carousel* Continuous Performance. Cissy and I never got to see it in any of its revivals; I can't remember why. The gum-chewing ticket lady in the glass cage examines me curiously as I push three quarters through the opening in the glass.

The theater smells of popcorn and faulty plumbing and of plush seats that never see light or a vacuum cleaner. The movie is in progress: enormous actors in full color and stereophonic sound play for a tiny audience of old ladies and sleeping drunks. In the dark my Coke doesn't quite connect with my lip; some of it drips down my raincoat and into my shoe. I wish I could cry, but somehow my head feels too solid and swollen to allow tears to escape.

I'm aware, now that my eyes have become accustomed to the dark, of a man in the seat behind me. He shifts in the seat, sighing, occasionally tapping the back of my seat with his foot. He rises and I think, good: this is where he came in. But instead of leaving he walks around to the next row and lowers himself into the seat next to mine. I glance at him. He's respectably dressed, hair neatly combed. He must be a lonely businessman from out of town, killing time until his appointment. Maybe he has poor eyesight, so he has to sit closer to the screen. He's eating gum drops from a cardboard box.

The virginal mill girls are singing about a clambake. The man's arm lies along the common arm between our seats and then—casually—his hand drops into my lap. His face still stares straight ahead at the movie, his jaw moving, softening the candy. Quietly I stand up, so as not to make a scene, and go up the aisle as though heading for the Ladies' Room. Instead, though, I leave the theater, wrapping my raincoat tightly around my body to protect myself from the storm.

The world must be full of men like that, smelling out my rampant sexuality.

The rain has begun again. In the street a gust of wind throws me out of balance, so that I scrape my cheek against a stone window ledge. Even the insult of pain fails to release the tears; the rain roughly soaks my hair and face. The feeling, which is closer to homesickness than anger or grief, seems concentrated in a burning sensation behind my breastbone. My white shoes fill up to the ankles in the rain water, which is spilling from eaves and running in dizzy pools across the sidewalk.

My garden is swamped. The zinnias balance at crazy angles; some bulbs have washed up and are becalmed in the mud. Trees creak and whine, lamenting their torn-off branches which lie everywhere, their white joints nakedly exposed. Water still pours along the gutters.

From the back porch I notice lights behind the dusty cellar windows. Nobody goes down there; it's only used for storage. I stand at the half-open cellar door and listen. Below there is a hollow, trickling sound.

"Somebody there?"

"It's me, Maurey. The basement's flooded, what a goddamn mess."

I make my way down the narrow, open-backed steps, ducking my head under the beam. A foot of water, dark and shivering, covers the floor, soaking into the stacked cardboard boxes, buckling them, and washing around threadbare upholstered chairs. The dim light from the overhead bulb, reflected, looks like a jellyfish hanging just below the surface.

"Where's it coming in?"

"Don't know, haven't figured that out yet." Pat's kneeling in the water under the steps, feeling around with his hands for the drain. "Ah, got it." He pushes aside the concrete slab and we watch while the standing water begins to be sucked down the hole.

"You know that big push broom in the back hall—bring it down like a good kid, Maurey."

"I'll tell Gran I'm home. Then I'll come help."

When I return with the broom, he's already paddling the water toward the drain with an old coal shovel. His trousers are rolled up to the knee, his shirt is knotted to the stair rail. The skin of his back glistens; his hair is damp with sweat. I leave my shoes on the stair, though they are already ruined, and lower myself into the water. "Ah, cold."

"Hurry up, all this stuff is going to fall apart."

We work together without talking, sweeping the water in waves crested with dirt toward the drain. A rolled rag rug surfaces, like the snout of some swamp reptile, and bits of cardboard and other flotsam drift by. "Look at the furnace, Pat. All those pipes and gauges. We're in the engine room of a submarine, like in an old war movie."

"A torpedo in the starboard."

"Another in the bow."

"We're fighting desperately to keep the ship afloat."

"The flag aloft."

The water level gradually lowers, leaving behind a layer of silt. A few uneven places in the floor still hold pools of water. "I think we've saved the ship, but my mother's going to have a fit. Those are her old love letters in that box."

I lean on my broom handle and laugh. "How do you know?"

"I read them. When I was a kid."

"Well, I understand that. I would have read my mother's, but there don't seem to be any. Maybe she burned them, who knows? Are these from your father?"

"No. From other guys, before she married my father. The old girl got around quite a bit."

The rain outside has stopped. Pat is inspecting the far wall, where the ceiling-height windows expose the roots of my ravaged garden. "Look, Maurey, this is where the water got in. Behind the drainage pipe, where the plumber chipped the plaster away to fit the new joint in."

"God save the plumbers' union."

"Thanks for helping me." His fingers touch the short hair at the nape of my neck. "Let's go upstairs and get washed."

Pat opens the door to the downstairs apartment and we go in, bare wet feet making tracks on the cold linoleum. His dog Hilda wags her bottom, licks our hands. The kitchen sink is full of dishes; newspapers and beer cans cover the table. Pat's jacket is lying on the floor.

In the bathroom light Pat notices the scrape on my cheek. He puts his hand on it. "Did you hurt yourself down there?"

I'd forgotten it. "Oh, no. Before."

He unbuttons my dress and washes me. Then he takes me to his mother's bed, before supper, before the streetlights come on to stay.

15

Marry me, Pat says, reaching away from me to pick up a pack of cigarettes from his mother's bedside table. It seems inevitable. By the time Peggy Meaghan arrives home from Shrewsbury, dropping suitcases and laundry bags all over the apartment, I have already changed the sheets, smoothed the chenille bedspread. Everything is all decided. Now I have only to let things happen.

There's nothing Mrs. Meaghan loves like a wedding. For as long as I can remember her sitting room has displayed a foot-high bridge doll in full regalia under a glass dome and her own wedding bouquet, embalmed and mounted like a trophy. Did she even notice when her husband ran off with the counter girl at Fannie Farmer's?

She sets up her sewing machine on the dining-room table and measures Cissy and me for dresses. She decides on Empire Style, Cissy being so pregnant. Fitting the pattern pieces onto Cissy's mint-green material, Peggy remarks, "I'm glad to see you finally putting a little meat on your bones, Maureen."

Cissy's eaten alive with curiosity about the whole set-up; she'd never even guessed Pat liked me, let alone wanted to marry me. Very tricky, and all that time she wasted feeling sorry for me and trying to find blind dates. To pacify her I let her in on a secret: Pat was the first man to kiss me. I smile. First and only, she's thinking.

The weather stays hot, though the field behind the school is turning brown in patches, and there are lunchboxes and school supplies on sale in Kresge's.

Peggy and I visit the cake shop across from the church, which also from time to time caters parties and weddings. We sit in the back room with the narrow-lipped Czech proprietress, next to the bread-slicing machine, and Peggy orders a wedding banquet of cold cuts, two kinds of salad, various hors d'oeuvres, a three-tiered wedding cake. The smoked turkey will be all sliced beforehand and then reassembled, boneless, on a styrofoam support. That's the specialty.

Gran accepts Peggy's taking charge with surprising good grace. She's feeling her age, arthritis worse in all her joints. She doesn't say much. When I told her about the engagement all she said was "It's a blessing," and let it go at that.

She doesn't go out to hunt for bargains or to play cards so often. Her friends' visits are nothing but organ recitals, she tells me. Patting the red loose flesh at her neck, she says, "Well, I wish I had Angie's veil to give you, at least. Real Limerick lace it was, hand-made and very costly, it being during the war and all. Frank Mullen had it ordered special for her through somebody he knew

in New York. Probably something fishy about it, but *I*
didn't ask. One day she just gave it away."

I'm dropping a cube of beef fat into the pan. I slide
the fat around with the point of my paring knife, slicking
the whole surface. Then the stew meat goes in. The smell
of singed meat is nauseating.

"Who did she give it to?"

"Nobody worth mentioning. Some ragpicker or
handyman. No, the spastic lady that used to come around
to the door selling notions—seems like it was her."

I remember that woman; once I shouted at her to tell
her Gran wasn't home. The memory makes me uncomfortable because even though the woman could only slob-
ber and drawl, probably her hearing was unimpaired. I
would like very much to know what was going on in my
mother's mind, after my father disappeared. What is my
connection to that poor person Angie Mullen?

"I thought maybe she gave it to someone she cared
about."

"She did care, some way, about those funny people.
Strays. But she just asked, 'What I need it for now, Ma?'
and I said, 'You could sell it, get a bit of money for it at
least,' and she said very soft, 'It wouldn't be right to do
that.' "

"That was true."

"Oh yes, she had very strong ideas about what was
right and what wasn't. A lot of good it did her."

Peggy unpacks her own lace tablecloth, polishes the
heirloom silver-plate cake stand, dispatches Pat and
Gowan off to the tuxedo-renting store in Central Square.
She wraps a piece of string around my finger, for size, and
puts it in Pat's pocket so he can give it to the jeweler when
he chooses the ring. She's on the phone with the florist

trying to decide between glads and mums for the altar. She's always very careful to keep me posted on the progress of the negotiations.

On a hot, hazy Sunday afternoon Pat and I go to the rectory to visit Father Smythe, who had been Pat's high-school classmate and is now in charge of youth activities and recreation. He uses his imitation Irish accent to charm the old ladies in the parish and then gets carried away: his voice bursts out and then, embarrassed, collapses in upon itself. His collar is stiff, his throat soft and razor-nicked.

"No doubt you young people have seriously considered this important step," he says, wagging the frame of his tortoise-shell glasses at me. I smile because he and Pat are the same age, but he doesn't seem to get his own joke. "Your mother tells me you've known each other a long time." Satisfied, he unfolds himself from the chair like a meter stick and gives each of us a booklet with a blue cover. "Bless you," he says.

On the street we open the booklets and discover they contain numbered precepts of marital advice. Pat laughs and drops the booklets into the first mailbox we pass on the street. "Oh, Pat." He is taller than I; he walks with an easy unconscious gait; his hair is clean. We're having fun as though playing a game. "He jiggled his eyebrows just like Groucho," I say. He takes my arm.

Pat touches me with a shy, proprietary air. He takes me around the corner to Vic's for a pizza—he knows the regulars there. The waitress leans over his chair to pour his beer and brushes his shoulder with her pointed breast. He gives her a friendly wink. Pat and I don't find much to talk about, but the jukebox is so loud it doesn't matter.

Sometimes Gowan joins us, and then he does most of

the talking. Everybody in North Cambridge knows him. He's always in the local papers, singing at wedding parties, Christmas concerts, political banquets. His voice is untrained, but he's not shy about it. It's almost as though his voice doesn't even belong to him but to his mother, because she taught him the songs.

He lived with his mother in an apartment on the Somerville line ever since he was a small child, and after she died he just went on living there. He often talks of moving, because he doesn't need so much room any more, though that parrot Seamus scatters birdseed in every cranny, a fat arrogant bird.

Gowan is a sort of amateur local historian. He understands the way that personal connections are nearly as complex as the networks of electric wires or sewer pipes laid out in the neighborhoods. He knows whose cousin is married to whose aunt, who is expecting and who has taken the veil or taken to drink, whose fortunes are rising and whose falling. Who has died and how many Mass cards received.

All these odd, fragmented families, members missing—lost, or moved, or strayed, or on the other side of the Atlantic—it's old maid's work, keeping track of them.

He never mentions Charlie. He talks about his mother, who came over from County Meath in 1931 to marry a man she'd never met. "My father was a friend of her cousin's; they worked in the same factory, and he got my mother to exchange letters with him. It was a little tool factory." As if that reminds him, he takes out a pipe tool and digs into the bowl of his briar. The pipe is something new, maybe an affectation to impress the chicken-farm widow. Charlie would enjoy the joke.

"The depression was on, Maureen. Nobody had any money. When I was a child my mother took in other people's children, so they could go out and work—it always seemed that I had lots of brothers and sisters, though I was an only child. After my father died, she did other jobs too, knitting sweaters for people in the evenings and turning their sheets. Cutting the sheets down the middle and sewing them together again so the worn places would be on the outside edge."

Pat gets up to order another round of beers.

"I hated that, Maureen. All those sheets from other people's beds, smelling of their bodies, draped around the house all the time."

It's strange that both Mick Gowan and I are orphans—if you can talk of a grown-up person as being an orphan. There's something rudderless about it, frightening, difficult to explain to other people.

"How did your father die?"

"An injury at the factory began it; his left hand was mangled in a machine for stamping tool parts out of metal. He was a lefty; he was always a little out of sync with things. They said he'd been drinking on the job, so he only got a very small compensation from the company. After that he just drank—very quietly, never bothered anybody. He died of pneumonia in 1941. I remember the date because it was the same month as Pearl Harbor, just before Christmas, and a boy on the block enlisted in the Navy. That boy had been a special friend of mine."

"Did he come back?"

"Oh, he did. He came home with a Samurai sword in a long wooden box, said he took it from the body of a Japanese officer killed in hand-to-hand combat, but I bet he bought it in some Yokohama pawnshop. He's got six kids now, lives in Chelmsford."

"Have you been in Yokohama, Michael?"

"I was there on leave, on my way home from Korea."

"Don't start him in on that," Pat says, sliding the beer glasses across the table.

Gowan swallows his beer quickly and then leaves, giving us a benevolent smile. It's only then I remember that Pat is fatherless too—but it's different if your father just takes off with some girl. Pat is drinking his beer without apparent concern, no bitter memories to spoil the taste. He searches through his pockets for a coin to put in the jukebox. It's comforting, in a way, to be marrying a person who doesn't feel things deeply. How calm everything will be.

We walk home from Vic's the long way around, and Pat kisses me in the foot tunnel under the railroad. Broken glass is gritty under our feet. I press my cheek into his jacket so that the copper button on the pocket makes a mark. The freight train on its way to Springfield rumbles over us. He says idly, "Wonder what we could collect if the train caved in on us."

16

Wednesday is Pat's day off. He borrows his mother's old gray Chevrolet and we drive to Purgatory Chasm for a picnic. He's a good driver. He doesn't talk; he turns on the car radio to a black rock station and smokes, flicking the hot ash out of the window. His elbow rests on the window frame. When I ask him to stop at a gas station so I can use the restroom, he stays at the wheel, letting the engine idle. It's Hilda, his dog, who watches me as I walk back along the grease-soaked asphalt.

While Hilda yaps after squirrels Pat makes love to me. We're rolled up in a blanket. He sticks his fingers through moth holes in the blanket and wiggles them to make me laugh. I love the smell of wild thyme crushed under us, but the image I bring home is of a cinder-block park stove in which the rain had turned the spent coals to tar.

I am awake most of the night, some nameless tension gnawing at me.

But by morning things look calm and ordinary again: Gran at the kitchen table playing cards, her cotton stockings hanging over the stove to dry, the sun in geometric patches on the linoleum floor. I sit in my nightgown until midafternoon, drinking tea. There's always noise on for company, soap operas or game shows.

I can't make up my mind whether to see Charlie in the hospital. On the table is the letter from McLean's offering me a job as staff nurse; there's a wrinkled brown circle on it where I put down my cup. A ward full of mad people and myself maddest of all. I can't answer it.

Crumbs wound up in webs of dust collect on the floor. As I sip my tea, I read every item in both the morning and evening newspapers, including stock reports, obituaries, long-range weather forecasts. Nothing stays on my stomach except toast with butter and cinnamon sugar. The cinnamon shaker is a ceramic begging bear; according to Gran, my mother sent away to a cereal company for it when she was eleven or twelve. The glaze is crackled with age.

Gran holds her tongue about my listlessness, though I know she's thinking about my mother. She tried to hide the begging bear, but I found it again behind some empty jelly jars in the pantry. Gran turns up the missing black seven but has forgotten where she needed it. I cut my hair with the dull kitchen scissors, not bothering to look in a mirror, and she clucks softly but doesn't make any remark. Waiting: for a wedding, a child, a death.

In fact, death does tempt me. I close my eyes and feel nausea; the room changes direction and whirls the other way. No point in dwelling on it, though. I know that in the end I'm too sensible to use a razor in those firm cross-strokes, the way my mother did. When I walk in the street the polly noses stick to my shoes; my awareness of them binds me too closely to the earth.

I wake up at two in the morning and think about Charlie, try to remember his face. I feel panic that I have forgotten it, and if that's true, there must be something horribly wrong with me. Perhaps I am incapable of love. How cool I am about Pat.

I lie in bed trying to reconstruct Charlie's face from the individual features: pale eyes, teeth just so slightly rabbitlike, skin shallowly pocked. But the pieces don't fit together very well. His exact image eludes me, like a word on the tip of the tongue.

Though I am exhausted, I can't relax enough to sleep. Hilda is restless too; she noses along the fence in the back yard, growling low in her throat at some imagined intruder. She sees my light go on and barks, a brisk snap. But I'm not coming down to chase away your bogey man, Hilda my girl.

I unfold the newspaper clipping. It's a group photo, printed in the *Chronicle* in mid-July. Near the front, because he is short, is Charlie O'Clair. His face is in three-quarter profile, smudged, flattened by the flash bulb, but at once I see the element that has been escaping me, that ties the features together. Self-confidence, maybe. No, desire is closer to it: wanting something badly that has nothing to do with classroom space or child-to-teacher ratio. He'd already had the cancer inside him when the picture was taken, early in June, but he hadn't known it.

For a long time I peer into the face in the clipping, so closely that I see it is actually composed of tiny dots, various shades of black and gray. The essence of him again escapes me.

In the same way he inched away from me those last few days before he went back to the hospital—there was something lacking in me.

I really must go see him, but I'm afraid. Probably he has no wish to be reminded of me now.

Seeing us, the neighbors smile, pleased. Pat and I sit together after supper in the grass next to the foot tunnel. He smokes, leaning on his elbow, watching the basketball players. There's a place on my ankle where a patch of poison ivy is dried but I scratch anyway. It's become a habit.

"Do you remember when I was a baby and we moved into the apartment above you?"

He scrubs the butt out with his shoe. "Yes, some things."

"My mother was with us then."

"Her name was Angie."

"That's right."

He discovers that the cigarette pack is empty, crumples it and tosses it onto the railroad tracks. "She had dark hair, but not like yours. Curly and thin and fixed up on top of her head. Kind of a jittery person." He's quiet for a while, watching the game. Then he says, "One time I do remember. It was my birthday; I was about five, I guess. There were balloons tied to all the bushes in the back yard, a lot of kids in party hats. My mother made us play a game, the one where a person is blindfolded and tries to find the other kids and then guess by feeling them who they are."

He's talking softly, sucking the juice out of a blade of grass. "Well, there was one little girl, God knows who she was, but she didn't know anybody. When it was her turn to be 'it,' she couldn't say it's Tom or Brenda, you know.

My dumb mother kept tying the blindfold back on her when she guessed wrong, and the kid was getting more and more upset, and your mother was watching all the time from the porch. Then finally your ma jumped up and ripped the kid's blindfold off and flung it up into a tree. It was a scarf, made out of some red material. It stayed there for years, it seems like, getting more and more ratty-looking, but every time I saw it I remembered her. Wondered where she'd gone. No one would ever tell me."

I am much struck by this, the vision of the tattered red scarf clearer to Pat than my mother had been. "Do you know now?"

"Sure, I figured it out later on."

"That's what I had to do too, bit by bit. I'm still working at it, trying to find her, but I'm scared of her too. Does it worry you that she was mad?"

"You're not like her." He lies in the grass. It must be uncomfortable, scratching his neck. Gnats biting. A plane overhead screeches as it turns in some holding pattern waiting to come into Logan.

"What do you remember about me, then?"

He laughs. "Is this a game?"

"Yes, a game."

"Okay, let's see. I remember my mother taking care of you when you were a little kid, giving you a bath in the kitchen sink, soaping all over you. I wanted to touch your slippery pink skin, but I didn't dare."

"Why not?"

"Maybe I thought my mother would smack me."

"For your dishonorable intentions?"

He rolls over and pulls a handful of grass, laughing. "They probably were. Your turn."

"One time in the summer we were playing with the

garden hose on the back lawn, you and Cissy and me. To shock us you pulled up the leg of your bathing trunks and shot a stream clear across the yard. You were very proud of yourself, but I thought it looked like a little curled slug."

He presses his body against my extended leg and I feel the hardness in his groin. "You know how to put me down, Maurey."

"They're waiting for you to play."

He goes off to the court, leaving me to guard his jacket, which is spread out on the grass like a sleeping man or a dummy. Some boys are in the underbrush by the tracks, trying to shoot birds with BB guns; I can hear the gentle *pop-pop* and their triumphant cries.

Later, Pat and I make love there on the damp ground, stuck by twigs. Tugging at my shirt buttons, he says, "You are not like I expected," but really, I don't think my lack of shyness surprises him much. He takes things easily, does not think a lot. We share a quart of ale, listening to the freight train clack over the tracks, like wooden counting beads on a child's wire frame. I'm glad of his company.

"Are you sure you want to marry me, Pat?"

"It's always been in the back of my mind that's the way it would be."

17

I turn the key in the ignition of the old Chevy, listening for the engine to catch. The floorboard is rusted out so that I can see the pavement through the clutch hole. The inside of the car smells of enclosed summer heat; a dying fly buzzes in the back window. The seat is stained with lipstick.

The car starts, bumping away from the curb. Driving it is like driving a mule from behind with a stick, the response only approximating the command. You have to turn the wheel very hard at a corner and still the tires take their time about turning, letting the car drift to the wrong side of the street.

Today's the day I get my blood test. Pat's mother insisted I take her car to the hospital, saying, "You are my daughter now." It's incongruous, that blowzy candy-cotton-haired woman holding a vacuum-cleaner hose—my mother. But also touching. She's always thought I am a little peculiar. Solitary, bookish, not to mention the prob-

lems with my ancestry. Like Pat, though, she's not a wor-
rier. She just opens a beer.

At the west end of Verdun Street, where it meets
Sherman, there's some kind of traffic block-up; the cars
are stopped in three directions. It often happens when a
train is passing the railroad crossing on Sherman and the
gates are down, or when somebody parks in the narrow
street near the corner. The Chevy keeps threatening to
stall while I wait in the line of cars and so I cosset the ac-
celerator with my foot, not paying any attention to the
reason for the delay.

A man driving the opposite way rolls down his window and shouts at me. "Which way you wanna go?"

I point my finger to the left, toward the tracks.

"Nah, turn right, go around the block. Nobody can
move."

"It's not my fault."

"Move. Ged oudda here."

I hesitate, then as the car ahead of me turns right, I
follow it, although I'm going in the wrong direction; I'll
be late for my appointment. I park by the side of the road
for a few moments, waiting for the blockage to clear. I
sense my baby ticking under my heart like a tiny clock.

Strange, unexplainable hostility. There's no way that
man can know what I have done. The baby is so vulnerable. Every day I'm tied closer to Pat.

The technician in the lab, a duffer, a man with large
pores and oily expression, jabs the inside crooks of both
arms half a dozen times to find a workable vein. He complains all the while about people with tiny hidden veins,
deliberately making his work tough for him. Bruises are
already forming by the time I decide to go upstairs to see
Charlie.

He's lying on his back, drowsing uneasily; I have a

moment to gauge his condition. They have him thoroughly guyed down with wires: intravenous dextrose and vitamins going into a cut-down in his forearm, nasal catheter for oxygen dangling over the head of the bed, urine catheter draining into a graduated bottle. His skin is loose and sallow. The student at the nurses' station told me, "We don't know how he's hung on so long," and the awkward way his head is thrust back on the pillow does seem like the broken neck of a hanged man.

I sit in a straight chair next to the window; the slight creaking of the chair legs and the sound of my clothes awakens him. He is blinded by the sun, which is sliced by the venetian blind behind me. He shades his eyes with the untied hand, waiting for me to speak first: I might be only an hallucination.

"Hello, Charlie."

"Where have you been?"

"I wasn't sure you wanted me to come."

"I asked my wife to call you."

"I didn't get any message."

"She forgot, I suppose." His voice is shocking, all in the mouth. The cancer must have gotten to his throat, too. As I pull the blind cord, dipping the slats, he notices the blood-soaked bandage in the crook of my arm. "What happened to you?"

"Just a blood test. The lab man botched it up."

"Are you sick?"

"No. Just one of those routine things."

He thinks about that for what seems like a very long time; I'm reminded of his concentration over a mathematical game or a chess problem or a question of political maneuvering. Only now his reflexes are so much slower.

"Wouldn't that be only a prick of the finger?"

"Well, all right, why should I lie to you? It was a marital test. They have to take a lot of blood for it."

The sun now makes bands of light on the floor. There is a dense smell of roses, many bouquets crowded together on bedside table and windowsill.

"You are going to marry that boy, that shoe salesman."

"We've known each other so long. Everyone expected it."

"You don't do things . . . because people expect you to." Though his voice is only a whisper, he won't leave the bone alone. "Why, Maureen?"

"You force me to say it. I have to marry." I snap the overblown blossoms out of the floral arrangements in the window and drop them into the wastebasket. "I'm pregnant, Charlie."

"Is he the father?"

"No."

"It's mine, then."

"I didn't want you to know." My voice is flat, and in the bed his body looks shrunken, ugly. He turns his face away.

"I want your child, Charlie."

"What can I do for you?"

"Nothing. It's too late."

Of course I mean my wedding preparations, already under way, and then I realize that it's his dying he's thinking of. He lifts his arm and feels the tug of the IV catheter. He opens his hand and closes it, as though he never noticed how those muscles worked before. "Look, Maureen." He kicks aside the sheet to show me the skin metastases, his legs now covered with blue-black lesions. "They're inside, too. My liver, heart, everywhere."

"Charlie, all I do is hurt you, it seems."

"Are you going to be happy with him?"

"I think so."

"Does he know?"

"Not yet."

"Don't tell him. Promise, Maureen."

Already I'm thinking about going. "All right."

"I don't want to have every part of me die." He reaches out to touch me, but I draw back. I'm sensitive of my belly, protective of the child.

"I have to do some shopping. Gran will be wondering what's become of me."

"Will you come again?"

"I'll try."

In the visitors' corner, between the telephone booth and the elevators, I see his wife sitting in an easy chair, reading a magazine. She could be waiting for the hairdresser.

I'm worn out by his intensity, his suffering. And yet I'm strangely uninvolved, as though I have been watching characters in an afternoon soap opera. I have already imagined him dead and accepted it.

18

Uncle Frank smells equally of gardenia and dry-cleaning compound in his formal black suit, more frequently used for funerals than weddings in recent years. He leans on my arm, rather than the other way around, and waves the imp-headed cane under the dimmed chandelier. Behind the altar is the stained-glass portrait of the crucified Christ.

The wedding march begins. The guests come raggedly to their feet, stretching their necks to see the parade; Cissy in her ballooning green dress marks the pace. Pat's at the altar, rocking slightly from heel to toe, casual, as though he left his cigarette burning in the vestry and expects shortly to go back to it. Gowan is there too; he's the nervous one. His trousers are wrinkled around the knees.

My ankle itches. I'm thinking, absurdly, that if at this moment Charlie rushed in, dangling catheters from all orifices and demanding that the ceremony stop, that, yes,

I'd go away with him. But the music pulls Uncle Frank and me ahead, and in the front pew Pat's mother is turning toward me, smiling a welcoming smile.

Only one tree on Verdun Street has leaves turned gold and scarlet, but it is a broken, diseased tree, and for some reason the leaves on its dying limb turned first. Insufficiency of nourishment, or something like that. The air is cold; a milky cloud floats above the old paper mill.

The delicatessen is spread out on Peggy Meaghan's dining table, arranged on assorted plates, crowded over the lace tablecloth. Uncle Frank, in his element, forces slices of the predissected smoked turkey on the guests; the champagne is opened with pops and cries. Cissy has little Ronny dressed up in a red velvet suit with matching bow tie, his hair barber-cut and slicked down. He toddles between the ladies, clutching an increasingly soggy petit four. Gran, solid in her diamond-patterned purple rayon dress, piles the paper plates with deviled eggs, macaroni salad, midget sweet pickles, potato chips.

Gowan strikes the rim of his glass with a fork and there's a hiss for silence. He raises the toast to the bride. As is the custom, he's dug up an old story about me. One time he tried to sell me a pair of shoes. And I'd said, "The wearer knows best where the shoe pinches." A clever girl, Maureen. Well, she'd got herself a husband good at pinching. General laugh. Ah, Gowan says, but a girl who can tell what's best for her, as her choice of Pat as a husband proves. Applause and champagne bottles passed all around.

I'd forgotten the incident. I suppose I was thirteen or fourteen, deliberately trying to bait the simple shoe salesman with that old saw. Funny of Gowan to remember. Embarrassing of him to tell it here—almost as though he knows I took Pat every bit as capriciously as I might buy a cheap pair of shoes. Gowan's not so simple.

The wedding cake is unveiled: three rose-studded tiers, capped by a plastic bride with painted cheeks and a grinning though somewhat wall-eyed groom. Cissy holds my bouquet as I cut the first slice, my hand under Pat's. I smile for the photographer, feeding a bite of cake to my new husband, but my eyes are closed the moment the flashbulb goes off. Pat stuffs some cake into my mouth and again there is applause. The icing is stiff, like plaster, and the taste perfumed.

We pose for more shots, Peggy now in charge. The photographer's name is Haring and in fact he does look like a little fish, with his rubbery mouth and exophthalmic eyes. He's been courting Pat's mother for years, fruit-lessly so far, but as a favor to her he's doing this wedding for half price, candids included. "Smile, darling," he begs me; my jaw already aches with smiling.

More champagne is poured and the bottles of whis-key are broken into too. Gowan kisses me, and Uncle Frank, and Mr. Flynn, the next-door neighbor. And then Vince Ranelli takes my arm and says, "Don't I get to kiss the bride?" I lift my cheek, but he plants his whiskey-wet lips on my mouth. "There's something funny going on," he whispers.

"Don't be stupid, Vince."

"Oh, but that's what Cissy says. She says the whole thing was arranged so quick, and how come? I mean, she's hurt you won't tell her anything."

"There's nothing to tell."

"C'mon, Maureen. I just wanna be, what you call it, *simpatico*. Like those fancy pols you hang out with." He's got hold of my arm and I look around for Pat, but he's on the other side of the room telling jokes to his mother's friends. People have begun to dance to the phonograph.

And then Uncle Frank pokes his head between us and sucks in his denture. "You should be dancing, Maureen. You and Pat."

"Butt out, old man," Vince says.

"What?"

"Butt out, I said. What's the matter, you deaf?"

Uncle Frank, enraged, hesitates only a second. All of a sudden he's Cyrano de Bergerac. He winds up and thrusts the tip of his cane into Vince's ruffled lavender paunch. Vince's eyes pop; he loses his balance and staggers backward, sitting squarely on the platter of deviled eggs on the banquet table. Meanwhile, Uncle Frank topples the other way into a gaggle of Peggy's friends. Champagne trickles down his face and onto the funeral suit.

There is a moment of silence. Then Pat says from his seat on the radiator cover, "Well, I've heard of egg on your face . . ."

"My tablecloth," says his mother.

"Glory be to God," says Gran.

November: a few dry snowflakes falling. I find out about Charlie's death, sooner than I expected, by coming across his obituary in the newspaper. No photograph—a man of only middling importance. A member of defunct local committees, a man who aspired to great things but never quite made it. Helen O'Clair née Hanlon, the sole survivor. Funeral services are to be private.

19

Pat is an easy man to keep house for. He's not the sort of man to become hysterical over an empty sock drawer—instead he picks up a dirty pair from the floor and wears them another day.

In November, only a few days after Charlie's death, Pat and I move into our first home—an attic apartment in a three-family house on Winter Street, off Montgomery, around the corner from the lumber yard. We've been under Peggy's flapping wing for nearly six weeks while we searched for a place. There are not so many belongings, packed into supermarket boxes and shopping bags; a few trips in the Chevy takes care of the move. Our clothes, still on wire hangers, are laid on the bare mattress ticking in our new bedroom. The box springs are set on conical screw-in legs, no head or footboard.

There is something almost unbearable about the sight of my last year's Easter suit, Pat's winter coat, his trousers with hanger creases running the wrong way, the dress I wore to Cissy's wedding, my old pleated skirts from high school, the student uniforms, all in indiscriminate piles half sliding to the floor. They symbolize distress more than anything else, these objects that are like former selves, all scrambled.

I open a living-room window and let the raggedly hemmed nylon curtain flutter against my cheek. The day is icy, the leaves down except for the stubborn withered oak leaves still hanging on. The sky is like the inside of an oyster shell.

In the front yard are a pair of hydrangea trees, their branches cut back to the knobby stumps in preparation for winter. I watch Pat bringing in the last odds and ends (a lamp, a wastebasket, an iron with a dangling cord) from the car, kicking the door shut with his foot. Hilda sticks right with him; she's frantic with the idea that all these things displaced might spell some unimaginable doom for her. When they come in, I pull a beach towel out of the top of a shopping bag and fold it so as to make a nest for Hilda under the stove.

"You show it to her, Pat. She won't believe me it's okay."

I open the refrigerator door and am offended by the odors of the former tenants, though the landlady has evidently made some effort to clean it out. I drop half-empty jars of pickles, mayonnaise, grape jelly into a garbage bag.

"Hey, maybe we could use those," Pat says. "They got mold in them?"

"They aren't brands I like."

"Jesus."

"Well, try to understand. It would be nicer to start fresh, with our own things."

He shrugs, opens a beer. He whistles to the dog between his teeth, kneels down, pats the towel. Hilda turns round and round on it, sniffing, suspicious. "Women," he says.

The apartment has four rooms and a bath, all with sloped ceilings because of their position under the eaves, all sparsely furnished. The floor is made of large squares of brown linoleum laid over plywood, not even nailed down, overlapping in some places, curling up in others. We have a long and narrow sitting room in front, over-looking Winter Street; a dark kitchen with a home-made wood counter, covered with oilcloth, propped up against the deep sink; a bedroom with a closet made of sliding doors that are stuck in a half-open position; a second bed-room hardly bigger than a shoebox.

The main stairwell leads up to a central hall in the apartment, and even with the doors closed we can hear the boys in the apartment below playing hockey in their hall, pucks chewing up the woodwork. The back stairs wind down from the kitchen to the back yard. On the landing the boys' cat has its litter box. The attendants in my mother's madhouse would have called the cat "untidy"— it regularly misses the box altogether. In front of the kitchen stove the floor creaks and sags. I imagine myself appearing some day without warning in the second-floor apartment, dusted with plaster, still clutching a spatula.

It's not so bad, though. I'm warm and the morning sickness is gone. I'm left alone most of the day, sewing curtains for the baby's room by hand, watering my house plants, reading, in the late afternoon starting supper. I call Gran to check on her or go around to play a hand of cards.

Aware of the slight swelling in my abdomen, I feel completed, like two interlocking pieces of jigsaw puzzle. I am often reminded of my mother, Angie Mullen, sitting in the furnished room in Watertown. I'm satisfied that, like her, I have already experienced love and death.

But, unlike her, I will not need to lose track of reality.

The child, unborn, is perfectly cradled and contained. Pat is gentle and familiar, tries to please me. He brings home a basket chair that was half price at Kresge's, with a wild story of his adventures with it on the rush-hour trolley, and he washes up the pots and pans after supper.

We each, unknown to the other, hire a different milkman, one at the back door and one at the front. We don't have the heart to fire either one of them. So we get milk and eggs at the front door and milk and ice cream at the back door. We envision some terrible dawn when both milk trucks arrive at once, and a terrific battle over territory is played out in the yard.

Pigeons live under the eaves, on the other side of the drywall. We lie in bed and listen to the birds cooing and squabbling in their nests for a few minutes after the alarm goes off—there are still stars in the sky; it is nearly the winter solstice—and Pat burrows his face into my night-gown, his head under the bedspread. But I move away, drop my feet to the cold floor, light the burner under the percolator. By the time the coffee is bubbling into the glass nipple, smelling better than it ever tastes, he's already in the bathroom, squeezing shaving cream into his palm and applying it to his flushed, unmarked cheeks. From the kitchen window the chimneys and aerials are odd, shadowy shapes; the radiator pops and bangs.

The strange thing about sex is that I think about it so little. I am like a bare-branched tree in its resting period; the baby inside is all I need. I'm happy enough.

I can easily take in Pat's body, swallow him up almost, and yet my mind moves clearly and lightly to other things: the match of thread to fabric (does it come out lighter or darker when unwound from the spool?), or the sound of ice-coated twigs tinkling on the window glass. I never come to orgasm. Pat doesn't seem to notice, but there's still a scrap of guilt about cheating him. Should I tell it to Father Smythe, who sits pulling his nose in the Confessional? Father, forgive me, for I have sinned. I suppose he wouldn't care either. He'd give me no penance, so long as I am producing a child for the Church. After Pat sleeps I move away from his moist body and lie looking at the winter sky, wondering why it's lighter than a summer sky.

Pat and I walk to Mass together and afterward buy a bag of pastries and the Sunday newspapers. Walking toward Rindge Avenue, I can see Charlie's house and, if I squint my eyes, the fat white teapot on the windowsill where I left it. Sometimes I wonder if his wife sees me. There's been comment in the neighborhood about her. They say she's always sitting in the upstairs window, staring down at the street with her tiny piglike eyes. Perhaps she's looking for me. I shiver, holding the warm, sweet-smelling bag of pastries against my chest. I take Pat's arm to cross the street.

In our apartment, Pat and I sit together on the braided rag rug and read the Sunday newspapers, starting with the comics. We remember the times Pat's father read the Katzenjammer Kids and Prince Valiant to us when we were children, as though we were brother and sister. Perhaps it didn't happen often, but we loved remembered rituals, invent them when they didn't exist. The air is hot and dry; coffee-cup rings and pastry crumbs collect on the maple-finish table. In the late afternoon Hilda and I nap on the sofa, the dog's back arched in the crescent below my abdomen. When I awake the apartment is dark and I realize that Pat has gone out somewhere, to see Gowan or to buy a beer. The room smells of old cigarette smoke. My cheek is impressed with the sofa's waffle texture.

I go to the kitchen to make myself a grilled-cheese sandwich, and Hilda sits up and begs for bits of cheese.

There is, in fact, more than a scrap of guilt about cheating Pat.

He's rewiring a lamp, and I nearly say, the baby's not exactly yours, you know. Casually I'd say it, as though it must be obvious to him. But he doesn't seem to have bothered to count up, maybe he doesn't realize how long it takes to make a mound of belly.

I rehearse to myself what would come next. Charlie needed life so badly, I had to help him. I didn't really want to.

Lightning would strike me at those words. Start again. I loved him for a few months; I've loved you all my life.

More *donner und blitzen*, like in the Katzenjammer Kids. He's screwing the wires into the new plug; his hair flops down over his forehead.

Oh Pat, nurture is more important than nature; if you play the father's role, you'll be the father sure enough. Could I say it convincingly? He might throw every stick of furniture out of the window and me on top.

He wanted me to marry him, insisted on it, kept me in his mother's bed lying under his body until I agreed. Yes, but he didn't know I was carrying Charlie's child inside, secretly nourishing it. I should have told him right then. But I was so exhausted; it just seemed simpler not to think, to let Pat have his way.

And I promised Charlie not to tell him. Perhaps the best thing is to forget. If I can.

*   *   *

Just as I reach Dr. Glass's office the parking-lot lights are coming on—five o'clock. Over the ragged bunch of weed trees that occupy the boundary between the lot and the car wash, I see one star. By reflex I grope for a wish and then realize it's probably a planet, that early and bright.

Dr. Glass pokes a cleaner into his pipe stem, jiggles it in and out, examines the end. "So you're pregnant already?"

"I'm five months along." I open my coat. "Can't you see?"

"Ah."

"Do you want me to tell you about it?"

"We both know where babies come from." He blows hard into the pipe stem to dislodge some inner obstruction. "Go see an OB and right away. Here's a list."

He won't be an accomplice in the fraud. There's nobody I can tell; I shall have to keep the secret to myself.

20

I haven't seen Cissy since my wedding day. I keep meaning to go around; it's unfair to let her think I blame her for the great deviled-egg fiasco. In fact, Pat and I like to laugh about it; he's sorry that was the one candid the little fish Haring missed. It would have put the finishing touch on our album.

I take the trolley and the bus to Inman Street, sit in Cissy's kitchen while we wait for the water to boil for instant coffee. On the table are scraps of felt and sequins, bits of wool. Cissy's making sock puppets for Christmas presents; she got the idea out of a magazine. "God, look at the bags under my eyes, Maureen. I can't see straight." Cissy has eleven nephews and nieces at last count. She's sewing on a button nose. Ronny squats under the table, hammering the floor with a toy gun. "Ka," he says. She passes a cookie down to shut him up.

"You know, I didn't want to butt in on your honeymoon."

"What honeymoon? One night in a motel and then back to his old room. Dark squares on the wallpaper where his centerfolds used to be."

"Well, at least he took them down."

"I don't know, I suspect his mother did."

She laughs, but I can tell that she's speculating about my body, under the loose brown jumper. "I'm dying to see your new place."

"It's okay, nothing fancy." I reach down inside my sock to scratch my ankle. My hair is wind-ruffled and flecked with melted snowflakes.

"God, you look about twelve, Maureen."

"Well, in spite of that, I'm going to be a mama."

"You work fast, you two." The kettle's boiling, the steam collecting on the windows, the outside world fogged away.

I wish I could talk to her.

She pours water into the mugs, stirs up the coffee powder into a thin brackish mixture. She bites into a cookie. "When are you due?"

"April."

I can see her counting backward rapidly; she was never as good at math as at this particular calculation. "Well, it's a nice month, anyway. I'm so scared of falling. I hate the miserable ice. I get so enormous I can't see my feet, and then it's just a puny six-pound kid for all that trouble."

All that trouble. The muscles in the back of my neck tense. I remember having to manage women in drugged hysterical labor when I was a student. I can't imagine letting go that way. Maybe Cissy can give me some hints about what the pain will be like, how to cope.

But there's something about her face, thin and sallow, freckled, the green mascara sad in this Inman Street kitchen, that keeps me from asking. I'm as old as a rock compared to her.

"Maureen, remember when we made pies out of choke cherries and flour in the old playhouse?"

What's she leading up to?

"Weren't we nuts? We thought we could bake pies in the sun. I think about that when I make a pie for Vince. I mean, how crazy we were."

"I'll say." I pick up my coat.

"Maureen, I'm sorry about the scene Vince made at the reception. He gets nervous about his job sometimes, and then he drinks a lot."

"Every wedding needs a riot."

"What did he say to make your uncle so mad, anyway?"

I shrug. "Who knows?"

"It's a pain. The cleaner couldn't get the grease out of his good trousers."

Passing the O'Clair house on the trolley, I notice that boxes full of discards have been put out on the sidewalk for the trash collection. All of Charlie's things, probably, no longer required. Snow is falling into the boxes. The corner grocery is selling Christmas trees, their branches bound tightly down with ropes, stacked against the plate-glass window outside the shop. There's an illuminated Santa, just his head, in the insurance-office window.

Hilda has become unhinged because of the move. She keeps wandering back and forth between Winter Street and Verdun Street, unsure of her true home, sniffing every fireplug and sapling, nosing papers in the gutter, as though she could read some sign there. Pat says, "If you wouldn't feed her, Ma, she'd stay home," and Peggy says, "Mercy, I don't have such a hard heart. She scratches at the door and looks around for her old bowl."

"She's getting fat, eating twice as much."

"Well, if food's enough to fill her up, then God bless her."

I'm surprised at Peggy's insight, but then again it might be just some trick of speech, some folk saying handed down to her and unconsciously repeated. Peggy lights a cigarette and tosses the pack to Pat, then picks up her knitting. She complains about the everlasting damp. "Your grandmother's feeling it in her legs, Maureen."

On Sunday the teapot in the window is gone, probably put out with the trash. Christmas lights are blinking in the gray gloom, at the toy store and the funeral home, but no sign of life in Charlie's house.

The phone at the shoe store rings and rings. When Pat finally answers I can hear the huge industrial vacuum cleaner roaring in the distance. "Pat, I'm in Belmont, at the vet's."

"Maureen, what the hell?"

"Hilda was hit, near Rindge Avenue. The neighborhood kids came to get me, and I brought her over here in your mother's car."

"Is she hurt bad?"

"At first I didn't think so. She wasn't bleeding much; she licked my hand. But the vet says her spine is injured. She won't be able to use her hind legs to walk, and that's no kind of life for a dog, he says."

He swears and the vacuum cleaner is silenced. I imagine Gowan bending over the switch. "So what's he want to do?"

"Put her to sleep."

"Oh."

"But I said I had to call and ask you. She's your dog."

"Listen, you'll have to decide what to do. I can't."

"All right."

The only thing Pat ever says about her is "That dumb dog, she was always surprised to see her own footprints in the snow, every damn time." There is unbroken snow in the yard, which is why he thought of it, I suppose.

At the beginning of January there is a thaw. A fly appears in the apartment, bold and brassy, zinging from one room to another as though it planned to take over and occupy. I wonder how flies materialize with the least bit of warm weather: do they winter over in suspended animation, snug in the dark corner of a back hallway? Or is the theory of spontaneous generation true after all?

Cissy's baby is born, missing by two days the bonanza of freebies from the Cambridge merchants—a daughter, named Reba Estelle, after Cissy's favorite soap-opera heroine and her mother-in-law, in that order.

I talk to her on the phone. "How was the delivery?"

"Great. I was in never-never land during the whole thing. My you-know-what is sore from the stitches, though."

"Doesn't it scare you to let them put you under? What if something went wrong?"

"Well, let's face it: if it does, I definitely don't want to know about it."

I remember how Cissy always had novocain for all those cavities. Every Wednesday afternoon at the dentist after the neglect in her mouth finally caught up with her. Sitting in the waiting room by the hot-air register, I'd hear Cissy yell at the mere sight of the needle. That dentist was paid by the installment plan. Her father's probably still paying him off.

"Who does she look like?"

Cissy laughs. "My mother-in-law—yammering all the time. Maureen? She has a birthmark, though. On her neck."

The change in temperature germinates the flu. I lie in the unmade bed listening to the cyclical hum of the refrigerator, which seems to echo exactly the disconnected buzzing in my own brain. Pat's shoes have tracked mud on the rug; the problem of cleaning it is more intricate and energy-consuming than I can manage. I'm flippin' out. Putting it in a silly slangy way somehow revives me. There's a gentle wind, and the children on the sidewalk are chanting, one-potata, two-potata.

Late afternoon, Saturday. Pat's at his mother's house watching a pro football game on TV. I'm restless, bored with the crumbs in the bed. I put on two sweaters and then my corduroy coat. When I glance at myself in the mirror by the door, I see that my hair is unbrushed, my cheeks mottled red and white. I run my tongue along the inside surfaces of my teeth.

Opening Peggy's back door, I hear the muffled enthusiasm of the sports announcer behind two walls; Peggy moved the set into her bedroom after Pat and I were married. I stand in the doorway of Peggy's room. There are the familiar pink plaster walls and on her dressing table the statuette of the Virgin, a bouquet of plastic roses and ferns, the carnation bath oil somebody gave her for Christmas.

Peggy is smoking in her upholstered easy chair. Pat and a girl are sitting on the chenille-covered bed, watching the game; her skirt, spread out on the bed, just barely touches Pat's hand. The girl turns. Her black hair is stickily bouffant, her face so soft as to be almost featureless, her eyebrows thin as arched new moons. I back off and tap the door shut with my foot; no one except the girl has seen me.

The walk home goes like this: up to the end of Verdun and right on Sherman Street, past the B & B Auto Body Shop and across Rindge Avenue at the light (that's where Hilda was hit), catty-corner to Montgomery. Three blocks down, the gray three-family house on the right, on the corner of Winter, the one with diamond-shaped panes in all the first-floor windows and two hydrangea trees in the front yard. It's strange how those furrowed stumps look different, on different days: sometimes like clenched fists, other times like club feet, or the leg bones of a huge prehistoric bird.

By morning the weather has turned cold again, the mud hardened into ridges and ruts. Out of some shared perversity Pat and I skip going to Mass and take Peggy's car to the Franklin Park Zoo. Pat doesn't believe in maps, and I refuse to stop and ask directions. We drive around the sooty slums of Roxbury, dead-ending in alleys and making false starts into the Arboretum before hitting the Zoo by accident. The sky is as gray and cheerless as an army blanket. I'm out of sorts, nursing my cold.

No cars are parked outside the Zoo gate. The wind is bitter, but when Pat reaches for my hand, I shrug him off. The paths are empty. Only the hooved animals are brave or senseless enough to leave their hay-filled houses and come to the fence to greet us; their coats are the same mud color as their compounds.

Pat's reading a sign. "Listen to this. A giraffe's

tongue is a foot and a half long." But they aren't demonstrating their remarkable organs today; they look mournfully into the bare tree branches, probably wishing they were back in Africa.

He has a curious way of walking, a lope really, with his left foot turned slightly out. I've noticed this before, but for the first time it annoys me, his casual bobbing gait. He stops and strikes a match inside his cupped hand to light his cigarette, inhales freely. "Lorna said you were at my mother's yesterday and then ran away."

"I didn't run away. I didn't care for the scene, that's all."

"What scene? What are you talking about?"

"Try not to be stupid, Pat."

"Look, Lorna's my mother's friend, her goddaughter's cousin, or something. I didn't know she was going to be there."

My throat is tight and sore. "You begged me to marry you, in that same pink room."

"I don't understand why you're getting so excited. I didn't *do* anything."

"I'm frozen. I wish we hadn't come."

"Okay, we'll go home then. But first let's see the elephants; you can warm up in there."

We come to a round stone tower, which is as deserted here as it would be on some wild heath; the stubbly grass is stiff with frost. The elephant house, Victorian and decaying, stands on the opposite side of what would be the Green if there were a single green thing in sight.

"I have to go to the ladies' first." I leave him leaning against the tower, sucking on his cigarette. He looks unconcerned—and even pleased. I walk back down the black-topped path, the way we came. The restroom door turns out to be locked; the minor frustration makes me feel even less like returning to him. The whole thing is some male conspiracy.

A pair of wild horses put their necks over their pen rail to be patted. Their breath is warm and coarse. Tarpans, actually extinct. Reconstructed from throwbacks. I guess they're unaware of their unlucky ancestral history; they're hoping I have some snack in my pocket.

A candy wrapper blowing on the path startles them, or else they are just tired of me. Suddenly they dart to the other end of their enclosure and nose about in the untidy clumps of hay. I feel the baby's body moving gently under my jumper, like an air bubble in a plastic sack filled with water.

I follow the winding path downhill, toward the entrance gate, away from Pat. Again there is that tight knot of muscles in the back of my neck. Peggy calls it "wry neck," says it's nerves.

Now is the time. Before we are any more entangled, Pat and I. He could go back to his mother's; it's plain he wouldn't mind a lot, hardly even notice. I stop in front of the caribou, finger the pattern of their wire fence. "Got to get going." I'm talking aloud to them, but they walk aimlessly in their muddy pen, paying no attention to me.

I could go to another city, get a job in a hospital, leave the baby with sitters during my shift. Babies mostly sleep, anyway. I imagine it curled up in a wicker washbasket, never getting any bigger.

One of the caribou turns and bites his tail. I wonder why Pat wanted me in the first place. It must have been some trick I played on him without meaning to. I am not easy like his girls, like Lorna. There is always something sharp about me, like broken glass, like a cat's tongue.

Maybe it was my distraction with Charlie that interested him; during the summer he sensed something queer, sensual going on. Well, no, probably not. It was time to take a wife and I was handy. Gowan or his mother put him up to it. He never looked in my face to see what was there, or maybe, in fact, my face was blank. So damn calm on the surface, always.

When the baby is born he'll become the father, and that will be that. So many meals cooked and shirts ironed and sheets smoothed over, he'll be depending on me too much. I'm not up to it, that's all. My insides will become all mixed up with his. I'll be nothing.

The trouble is Gran. She can manage without me for now, but not for too much longer. I think of Gran's kitchen, teacups on the table. The fear of being alone, of being homesick, is already seeping through my coat like the cold sooty air.

The caribou drops to the ground, folding his bony legs under him and lowering his head under its weight of antler. He looks down his long nose and begins to chew over some old meal. Ruminating. Yes, bad habit I picked up from Charlie. And he never got away, either.

I turn away from the pen and walk rapidly uphill. Pat's still waiting for me by the tower. He only says mildly, dropping a butt on the grass, "What the hell happen, you fall in?"

21

I keep Charlie's watch in a box in the top drawer of my bureau. Not really my bureau but the land-lady's—it's missing half its knobs and the drawers stick in damp weather. Today it is raining, a thin Lenten shriving rain. Abstinence from sun.

Holding the watch to my ear, I listen to the delicate mechanism of cogs and gears beating—at the same rate, it seems to me, as the heart of an infant in utero. The smooth flat gold warms in my hand.

Pat's uneven step and tuneless whistle are in the stairwell. Home early for once. I slip the watch into the box under its blanket of cotton, but the drawer won't close. He finds me jiggling the drawer back and forth. "This stubborn thing." More irritation in my voice than I intend him to hear.

He gets a sliver of soap from the bathroom, pulls the drawer out, rubs soap along the tracks. He's fitting the drawer back into the bureau when he notices the box. "What you have in here?"

"You can look if you want."

He takes the watch in his hand, turns it over, puts his thumbnail in the groove and flicks open the cover to reveal the face, the spidery gilt numerals. "Where'd you get it?"

"Oh, Gran found it in some junk shop, I think."

"You keep it wound, do you?"

"I thought I could use it to time contractions when I go into labor."

"Doesn't your wristwatch work?"

"This face is bigger. Easier to see."

"Looks like it might be worth something."

"I don't think so. Only gold plate."

He snaps the cover shut and I put it back in the box. I feel relief and also scorn that he accepts the lie so easily.

April. I'm folding socks and underwear on the kitchen table and keeping an eye on Charlie's watch. The muscles in my abdomen tighten; I fill my lungs with air. Two minutes, forty-five seconds between contractions. The ache in my lower back hangs on.

Waiting for the doctor to get the message from the answering service and call back, I pack my toothbrush and nightgown into the old mottled cardboard suitcase. It has rusty buckles to keep it shut. Somebody once sent something to Gran in it; I used it to store doll clothes; later on I hid away poems and other abortive writings in it; I took it to the seaside when Gowan and Pat and I were there. One of those possessions that sticks to you like glue no matter how many changes you go through.

I clean under the burner rings on the stove. Odd: I never felt especially concerned about those hidden places before. All the plants get a dose of water and fishbone emulsion as if I'll be away indefinitely. In spite of the month, huge soggy snowflakes are falling. The bare tree branches make an intricate pattern against the woolly sky.

My heart's beating, louder than the lumber truck shifting gear, the church bells striking. The afternoon is gray and calm.

When I get the word to come to the hospital, I call Pat at work, Gran and Peggy on Verdun Street. Peggy rushes around in the old Chevy, her blond hair at wild angles from her head, her makeup awry. "So early, Maureen. Are you sure?"

Smiling softly, I slowly negotiate the two flights of stairs, my winter coat unbuttoned over my enormous belly.

The labor room is in the basement of the hospital. Subterranean. Blue-green walls, a dim quiet, waves painted on the wall, or do I imagine that? Seasick. The crashing all inside my ears.

The doctor's gloved finger thrusts up my rectum. Hard, stiff cervix. He smiles. "You'll be a good long while. Try to get some sleep." The nurse, a silent Filipino in long wrinkled gown and cotton skull cap, takes over. I'm now the victim of the woman-to-woman rituals: giving over of personal possessions, shaving of pubic hair, flushing out of the bowel. She winds a bit of tape around my wedding ring.

I doze between contractions. The nurse has transmuted to a Japanese. I am a prisoner of war, closed in a tiny closet with my acid-faced torturer. I wake to feel her head stethoscope pressing my abdomen. "Contraction now?"

"Yes."

"Good strong heartbeat."

She hands me a glass of orange juice. "You've only begun to dilate."

"I'm not going to have drugs, anyway."

"If you need, just ask."

Time is confused, each second dragging, but the hour hand abruptly jerking from number to number.

Willing myself to concentrate, I relax each muscle, one by one. But the gigantic uterine contractions are like an Atlantic storm in winter, waves suddenly shifting without warning, beating on me, tearing me open. My control is tenuous. The nurse is there with the needle; she seems fixed against the painted seascape on the wall, waving temptation. No. My voice is a whisper. The fear of nothingness is even worse than the pain.

I thrash, and the nurse pulls up the iron crib sides.

At dawn I am wheeled on a stretcher to the delivery room, up in the elevator. Windows here. The contractions ease off. For the first time in many hours I can locate myself in time, because of the spreading pink stain behind the hospital buildings. One of the windows is open; while my wrists are tied and my feet inserted into the stirrups I can feel a cool April breeze on my damp hospital gown. Somehow the air carries the smell of melting snow.

Then all at once the baby is determined to be born, or my body is bent on ridding itself of it. I push, push, in spite of a cramp in my leg and the doctor is urging, now rest, pant-pant-pant. The tray of instruments glitters. At the climax an explosive sensation like a cork out of a pop gun and then the creature is sliding between my legs, a slippery bluish animal encased in membrane with a convoluted cord dangling from it.

"A girl," the student nurses are saying. It cries, a faint mew, then a gasp and a louder wail.

"Is she okay?"

"Ten fingers and toes," the doctor says, laughing, kneading my abdomen so that the uterus will clamp up.

I lie in the recovery room. A nurse is shaking the girl on the next stretcher. "Wake up, dear. You had a boy."

"Oh no," the girl whines, "not yet."

"Yes, it's all over."

I am exhausted, and there is also a feeling of loss. A smidgen of understanding that the child is not part of myself after all, but another.

The child has straight black hair and a thin face with a cleft chin. To please Gran, she is christened Angela, after my mother.

She is a wiry light-sleeper of a baby who startles at a step or a moving pattern of leaves on the wall. When she cries in the night, Pat gets up and brings her to me to be nursed. There is a faint sweet smell of milk about us. Pat looks at my milk-filled breasts under my thin cotton nightgown. But he doesn't touch me.

22

There is a crack in the bedroom window, and Pat tapes a piece of cardboard over the pane.

I remember that he used to put pennies on the railway track. He laid them on the iron rails, and after the train went by there would be Abraham Lincoln's face flattened and made featureless like some poor person stretched on the rack. It was improper, sacrilegious almost. I'd stalk away through the milkweed, heading home. But Pat only laughed.

"Are you stupid enough to feel sorry for a penny?"

There was a small streak of violence in him. That was surprising, because otherwise he was placid and careless, shrugging things off.

Some violence is in us all.

Yes. But the point is he didn't notice the destructiveness in it, he just didn't feel it.

He feels things in a different way.

Maybe.

*   *   *

When I nurse Angela and she's greedily sucking the milk from my breast, my body relaxes and sensuality takes over. What I feel in my uterus is close to orgasm, but no one would give that name to it. It's as respectable, as classic as a Christmas card. I don't think of her father. Hardly ever.

Angela's head turns away from my breast when Pat comes in from work; her tiny body wrenches away from me, she arches her back. She awards the first smile of her life to him and he is only pulling off his muddy boots.

"How's my girl?"

"Let's hope she sleeps now. She fussed all afternoon."

Before she was born he made a cradle. Top-grade Ponderosa pine from the lumber yard around the corner, carefully sanded and finished. Tongue-and-groove joints, no nails, only a bit of glue here and there where things didn't quite work out. Her tiny head is black against the reddish soft pine.

He lifts her up, and she spits a little milk on his jacket. "Maureen." He reaches for me and his big body distresses me; he thinks that Angela is an extension of his own sexuality. I'm sorry for him. I give him a quick kiss and put a saucepan on the burner. We'll have eggs.

"She's smiling, Maureen."

"Could be gas pains."

After supper he's outside again, playing basketball alone on the concrete apron in front of the garage. I hear the sharp *splat-splat* of the ball bouncing, an endless uneven rhythm. Amazing attention span. He doesn't go over to the MDC courts any more, I don't know why.

When he comes in the ball rolls under the kitchen table.

"You look tired."

"I'm not, Pat."

"You don't ever tell me."

"There's nothing to tell."

"Are you worried about something?"

"The bedroom window. The cold air streaming in."

"Through the cardboard?"

I'm folding diapers on the table. Thirds like an envelope, then thirds again the other way. Her body is so small. "Yes, through the cardboard."

"I'll get a piece of glass and glaze it tomorrow."

"The landlady's supposed to fix it."

"God, Maureen, what do you want?"

I don't know what I want. In bed he digs away inside me and I'm like a field of clay, deep solid clumps of it. "Maureen, love."

I hate myself. I can give him no answer.

One time Pat and I walked in a wooded field near the dump. Everything was wilder and more rural then, and the dump was still being used, so there was a giant curl of acrid smoke over the treetops and scavenging seagulls. The gulls found our trash better pickings than the sea, I guess.

We were jumping over a shallow stream when Pat grabbed me and we slid together on the stones. A snake, he said. I was seven. Gran spanked me for coming home soaked. No snakes there, she said, disgusted. I suppose he saw a black stick, shiny with slime, under the rippling water. He would have been twelve.

I remember the coarse wet smell of his wool coat and the smoky smell of his mouth. Was he smoking already? Or maybe it's the dump I'm thinking of.

Another time we walked on the railroad ties, past the

back of the cemetery and the public-housing compound
and under a railroad bridge. A freight train clattered by;
the engineer in the cab waved to us. We came to a place
where a lot of old junk was abandoned. I found a wrecked
baby carriage, and Pat fixed the wheels to a fruit crate and
made a car for me. It had tin-can tops nailed to the front
for headlights and my initials M.M. painted on the side.
My initials are the same now.

Of course, Pat only played with me when Gran was
going to the hospital to see my mother, and she gave him a
quarter to look after me.

"That your brother?" a classmate asked me once.

"Yes," I answered.

It was a matter of prestige; everybody else had brothers.

I'm feeding Angela and Pat brings me tea.

"My mother got married when she was seventeen,"
he says.

"Did she? I thought you said she got around a lot."

"That was her first husband. My father came later."

"Oh."

"She was pregnant when she married the first time.
When they split up the kid went with the father. I have a
sister I've never seen, somewhere in Ohio."

He pours milk into my cup for me. "Sometimes I
think I'll get on a bus and go out there and try to find
her."

"Why don't you?"

He shrugs. I unhitch Angela from my left nipple and
transfer her to the other breast. Then I sip my tea.

"I guess I thought she'd be embarrassed to have me
turn up."

"Maybe we could go together some day."

"Yeah, some day." He sounds unconvinced. "I don't even know her name. It's hard to see a person in your mind when you don't know their name."

I can imagine her, though. Bleached coarse hair like her mother, ill-conceived. Jesus. Well, I'm not like Peggy.

"Wouldn't your mother tell you her name?"

"My mother talks a lot. But she's as secret as a cat."

When Pat picks up the tea tray the cups rattle together and one of the handles breaks off. He's always doing things like that.

"I'll glue it, Maureen."

"Never mind. It would only give way and dump a cup of scalding tea in my lap."

He goes out to the kitchen with the tray and I know I should call after him. "Pat, I love you." I do feel love for him. I think it's love. But my throat seems swollen shut.

"The hell," he said, dropping the cup into the trash can, hard, so that it breaks into a dozen pieces.

23

The shoe store is closed for alterations; workmen are tacking down new wall-to-wall carpeting and putting up Colonial-style paneling. Bring in a better class of customer, the manager says. Pat and Gowan secretly laugh. But anyway they get a four-day holiday.

It's been nearly a year since we went to the South Shore. This time we ride together in Peggy's car, and Angela's sleeping in my arms in the back seat. July, but the sky is overcast. Keeps the crowds away, says Gowan cheerfully, and Pat, having washed down his soft-boiled egg with a beer, is driving like a maniac along the Southeast Expressway. Luckily, the Chevy won't go very fast and the traffic's all going the opposite way on Thursday morning.

After lunch I carry Angela down to the sea. There are broken concrete steps leading from the sea wall to the high-tide line. The tide's coming in. A gray sky, no wind, no whitecaps, and the sea is gray too, darker toward the horizon. The baby and I sit on one of the steps. Bits of cork float on the water, coming in all the way from Portugal, I guess. The beach is deserted. When Angela wakes and whimpers I unbutton my shirt and put her to breast.

After a while Gowan comes down the steps behind me. He glances down at my bare breast and then looks quickly out to the water. There's a tanker moving slowly north on the horizon now.

"I'll leave you in peace, Maureen."

I wouldn't have thought Gowan would mind. Perhaps I am becoming too casual about my body. "No, don't go."

He sits on one of the lower steps, so that I can see his thin back and his sand-colored hair ruffling up from the bald spot.

"Maureen, have you heard the one about . . ."

"You don't have to entertain me, Michael." I say it gently, so as not to hurt his feelings.

"Where's Pat?"

"He went somewhere in the car. Maybe to buy beer."

The tide has reached the bottom step, almost lapping at his shoes. Seaweed's collecting on the rocks, heaps of it, black, with hollow floats like pustules. Gowan chews on his pipe stem.

"Pat's happier now that he's married."

"I guess you'd know if anyone would."

"What about you, Maureen? Are you all right?"

"I'm all right."

"I worried about interfering, bringing the two of you here last summer."

"Then you knew he was coming that day. It wasn't a surprise."

His low voice is almost washed away by the sound of the surf. "Yes, I knew."

You wonder about a man like Michael Gowan. When a man reaches forty there must be some reason he hasn't married. Opportunities gone awry. Apart from Charlie's joke about the chicken-farming widow, I know there have been girls he's courted. One was named Nina (rhymed with Dinah); she was a secretary at the county courthouse, some relation to Gallagher, the new city councilman. Though she had a wen on her forehead, probably she would have made a good wife. He just let her drop. Not that he ever tells me about such things; Gowan confides in Pat, and Pat talks about Gowan as though he's commenting on the weather or the Bruins win.

I've wondered if he's queer and doesn't realize it. Or maybe he does. It makes me feel sick to think of him in a public lavatory, one of those dismal contacts, picked up for approaching a minor, maybe. His name in the paper, his job lost. I wish he wouldn't wear ties that are so wide and shiny they almost cover his thin chest with decoration.

In the late afternoon Pat and Gowan go surf-casting under the low tin-colored sky. They come back to the cottage with a bucket of eels writhing in water, the black and silvery bodies intertwined.

"They're horrible, Michael."

He laughs. "No, you'll see how good they taste."

Pat opens a beer and sprawls in a wicker chair on the porch. The baby's sleeping there, a net over her car bed so the flies can't touch her.

Gowan and I are in the kitchen. He takes one eel

from the bucket and kills it by piercing the back of its head with a skewer. I can't help watching. He slips a rope around the eel just below the jerking head.

He ties the rope to a hook on the wall and makes a cut all around the eel's neck, right through the skin, rubbing salt into it.

I lean back against the icebox.

"Don't watch, Maureen."

"I've seen more than one grisly operation."

He takes a pair of pliers and eases the skin away from the body, below the salted cut. Then he pulls the skin down away from the head, slowly, slowly, like peeling off a very tight glove.

He begins to sing.

"She was a fishmonger, and that was no wonder, her father and mother were fishmongers, too. They drove a wheelbarrow through streets broad and narrow, crying cockles and mussels, alive, alive-o."

Pale eel blood runs on the counter.

"Michael, don't sing."

He looks at me, baffled.

"Not that song. Something else." I see Pat and Gowan and myself sitting drunkenly in front of the driftwood fire while Charlie is dying.

If Gowan understands, he doesn't say anything. He whistles another tune, something I don't recognize.

When I nurse Angela and feel her hair in the crook of my elbow, I remember Charlie's there.

Pat switches on the light. He's toweling himself off, rubbing his hair; it stands up as though he's had an electric shock.

"Gowan and I had a swim."

"In the dark?"

"Big fat moon out there now. High tide all the way up to the sea wall."

"You're crazy. You could have drowned."

"Not a chance. I wanted to wake you up and get you to come with us, but Gowan said no, you'd be too tired."

I lie in bed, waiting for Pat to turn off the light. This room is on the second floor of the cottage; the white ceiling is buckled. On one wall is a picture: a priest blessing a rabble of slum children. Michael Gowan is a pious man. He goes to Confession, Mass on Sunday, Matins every day during Lent. He was a choir boy, an acolyte.

I notice that the curtains are stuck to the rods with cellophane tape. He really does need someone to take him in hand. Maybe he should have been a priest.

"Gowan's a queer fish," Pat says, dropping the towel on the floor.

"What do you mean by that?"

"All those eels. Catching them is one thing, but eating them's another."

He's under the sheet now, leaning against me. His body smells of salt water and beer; his skin is still chilly and damp; his hair is making the pillow wet.

"I thought they were good."

"Did you?" He's happy and relaxed, lying on his back. "They tasted like grilled rubber boot to me."

I'm tempted to laugh, but damned if I will at Gowan's expense.

"Pat, why is Gowan your friend?"

"Why? I don't know. Friends kind of fall down from the sky on you."

Like wives.

The prices in the shoe store have gone up, all right. The store is now called The Bootery. But Pat's still bringing home the same old pay check.

24

I'm raking leaves in the yard. Crumpled saw-toothed ash leaves blown over from the tree next door, tangled in the chain-link fence and impaled on my bamboo rake. You can't burn leaves any more, on account of air pollution; they have to be stuffed into bags and left out for the trashman. I miss that sweet and sorrowful smell, the match put to the dying year.

Angela's sitting up in her carriage, buckled into a harness to keep her from falling out. She frowns, wrinkles up her face in suspicion when she sees Gowan. He hasn't been around for a long time.

"I came to borrow Pat's rucksack."

"Gosh, I have no idea where he's put it."

"He's not upstairs, then."

"No."

"Over at his mother's maybe?"

"I don't know where. He doesn't tell me where he goes."

I lift the rake to tear off the leaves bunched on its staves, and I look at Gowan's face. His gaze is short-sighted and perplexed.

"Can I give you a hot drink, Michael?"

"No, I won't stop. I'll hike while there's some sun." He smiles, but his voice is strangely flat.

Ever since the day he skinned eels, I can't see him without being reminded of Charlie. It's unsettling. I never grieved properly over Charlie. I never saw him dead. I unhooked all those nerve endings in my brain, but they won't stay numb.

He picks up Angela's red ball for her and walks away down the street. He doesn't see her toss the ball out again, petulantly, bored with him. Just as well. Gowan would probably stay there all day retrieving it for her and the crafty kid would only scorn him for it.

When Pat comes home he has under his arm a large suit box with a string tied around it. He can hardly contain his pleasure as I cut the string and open the tissue paper. Inside is a cocktail dress made of black silk with gold threads running through it.

"It must have cost a lot."

"Never mind how much it cost. Try it on."

The V-neck is so low that my white freckled chest is exposed; the gold threads smell of tarnish.

"The salesgirl told me she'd sell her soul to have it herself."

He wants me to look like a streetwalker, I think to myself bitterly.

"The dress is pretty, Pat. Only . . . it doesn't fit very well. Maybe I could exchange it."

"Never mind. Just throw it in the trash if you don't want it."

"Well, you can see yourself that it doesn't fit."

"I see that I can't please you, whatever I do."

I hang it in the closet. I know I'll never wear it; it will gradually slide along the pole, being displaced by my other clothes until it's behind the stuck door panel and he'll forget about it.

Putting a jar of baby food into a saucepan and running water around it, I hear Pat going down the back stairs. He swears at the cat box on the landing and slams the door. He doesn't come home until long after I've had my own supper and put the baby to bed.

Now I have to piece together Gran's finances, as well as my own. Gran always received two checks around the first of the month, the small annuity on her husband's insurance money and the government check for me. Gran would take them down to the bank and deposit them and then draw out enough cash for the rent, for the gas and telephone bills, the electricity, the church collection, the milkman and grocer. She never had a checking account. She'd take the money personally around to the various offices, make a regular day out of it: chatting with her friends, the clerks in the offices. She'd have lunch at the counter in Woolworth's or Kresge's and bring home some bargain knickknack.

Now, though, most of her friends have retired and she doesn't get out so much because of her arthritis. I send out checks for all her bills, have wrangles with the gas company, try to figure out where all the spare change goes. She's like a magpie, stowing things away.

Paying the rent again reminds me of the old days. Every Friday afternoon I'd have to bring the rent money downstairs and give the envelope to Mrs. Meaghan. Gran could never understand why I hated to do it, and I'm not sure I knew myself. I'd try to go down the steps quietly and just stuff the envelope under the door, but I'd nearly always be caught.

The door would open and I'd be sucked in. They had then a rented piano, a black upright with a cracked finish and one or two keys with the ivory chipped off. Pat took lessons. He had a good ear and an easy, imprecise way of playing. I had to be the audience. I had to admire that week's piece.

The piano stood against the wall where the maroon brocade sofa is now. I'd be made to sit in the deep arm-chair next to it, so low down among the musty cushions that I felt almost smothered. Light came into the sitting room, filtered through the bushes outside the porch and the venetian blinds—a strange light, drowsy and choked with sparks of dust.

His mother said he had a real ear for music. It was a mystery where he got it from; his father couldn't tell "Nola" from "Auld Lang Syne."

The shadows in the corners of the room were very dark and the smells in that part of the house unpleasant: carpet damp and wood rot and the ghost of some old stew. Also indefinable masculine smells; Pat's father was still around part of the time.

When Pat got to be as tall as his mother, basketball took over, and the piano was sent back to the instrument rental company. I don't think he ever touched a piano again. Writing out the check to give to his mother, I remember the dread I felt of bringing down the rent money, of sitting next to the piano as a suppliant, of being almost a part of Pat's family, but not quite.

November again. No snow has fallen to cover Charlie's grave.

*   *   *

The pigeons are cold and quiet under the eaves. I have been nursing Angela; if I'm lucky she'll sleep for another half hour before the alarm goes off. In the dark I feel for the flat cardboard box in the corner of my drawer. I know at once it's not there.

"Pat, what have you done with it?"

His arm is dangling over the side of the bed, his knuckles touching the floor. The blankets on him are all askew, the ends untucked.

"What?"

"The watch. My pocket watch."

His voice is casual and thick with sleep. "Sold it."

"Why? Why did you sell it?"

"I needed some money. It was the only thing I could think of."

"But you didn't ask me."

"You said it was junk. I thought you wouldn't care."

"No. It doesn't make any difference."

Angela, in her crib in the next room, has begun to cry, hearing our voices.

"It *was* junk, like you told me. They only gave me fifteen bucks for it, hardly worth the trip to Central Square."

The fool. Anybody at all can take advantage of him. My fault: my own lie springing back at me. I'd never find it again, even if I searched through all those crummy secondhand shops, every one of them.

"You'd better get up. You'll have to start for work early today."

"How come?"

I shut the bedroom window. "The trolleys will be running late. It's snowing."

25

When Cissy and I used to run up the back stairs and beg for toasted cheese sandwiches and cocoa with marshmallows, Gran would say, "What am I, a short-order cook?"

That's what I am now.

At the end of November I weaned Angela—a brief, bitter struggle—and went to work at Lenny's Grill and Carry-Out on Beacon Street. Lenny's is in that narrow wedge of Cambridge squeezed between the university and Somerville, an area where graduate students, garage mechanics and sagging old ladies live on separate floors of rundown houses. Arcadia, Eustice, Garfield streets. Nobody talks to anybody else; they are quietly waiting for Harvard to get around to swallowing them up. Most of the students couldn't talk if they wanted to—they are Chinese or African and seem very lonely. They fit my mood.

I leave Pat's supper warming in the oven at five and

push Angela in her carriage over to Gran's. Then I take
the trolley down to Porter Square and walk along Somerville Avenue, across the railroad bridge to Beacon Street.
It's already dark by the time I get to Lenny's, and he's got
the fat coming to a boil in the deep square tubs. My job is
to take the orders at the carry-out window and, when I
have a free moment, to slice tomatoes and onions or press
an English muffin onto the big dirty grill. Mary is the
other employee.

Mary is a big woman, even taller than I, with gray
hair and a voice that reminds me of the way the big bad
wolf imitates Red Riding Hood's granny—both gruff and
squeaky at the same time. She has big teeth, too, square,
dead-white and false. At first she terrified me. But she's
glad to have me around, because before I was hired she
had to do all the counter work plus the hamburger-frying
and washing-up of the dishes from the grill section of
Lenny's. So she's kind to me, in her way, and she tells me
about her children and their various disasters. Her daughter El dropped out of secretarial school and took all her
savings from working in a candy store in the summers and
went to Cleveland on a bus with an unemployed jazz mu-
sician.

"I finally moved yesterday," she tells me, unpeeling a
meat patty from squares of wax paper and laying it on the
grill. "My Lord, I don't know how I collected so much
junk. Tough area, glad to be out of it. I never got no sleep
at night or anything else."

"What about your daughter? Did you hear from
her?"

"No, and when she comes back, she'll get a shock.
She won't find her old room waiting for her."

Lenny, dipping a basket of fries into the bubbling oil,
laughs. "You'll give in, Mary. You always do."

"Huh. Her room's gone." She slams the patty into a

bun and passes it along to me to wrap. A squirt of catsup, a slice of pickle, a side order of slaw.

"Do you want something to drink?"

The young Chinese blinks at me. "Drink? No, no drink."

When I get home with Angela, Pat is asleep in front of the television set. His beer has tipped over and dribbled onto the rag rug. There's something repulsive about the back of his neck, colorless, like a bean plant germinated and grown without sunlight.

In bed, he wants to make love. My hair smells of the fish-frying grease; I can't bathe because there's no hot water left in the pipes at this hour. He's in and out of me quickly, then he sleeps again. Lying beside him, I worry about small annoyances: the mending I haven't got done, Gran's gas bill which is way too high—she couldn't have used that much gas in a year; the rust stains in the bath-tub; the library books that are overdue.

And I think about Charlie, remembering the calm white silence of his room. I wonder what my life would have been like if he hadn't died—if we'd been able to go on living together in that room. A stupid idea, of course. If he hadn't been dying, he wouldn't have wanted me.

It is sleeting against the window.

I walk around the apartment, bare feet on icy lino-leum. I pick up the phone and dial the weather, just to hear the sound of an ordinary untroubled voice. ". . . snow showers clearing by morning, followed by . . ." I look into Angela's room and in the dim light from the hall try to see Charlie's face in hers. I can never quite find him there.

Lenny's Carry-Out is not far from Gowan's house; he lives on Arcadia Street and now that he knows I'm working there, he comes around and orders a late supper just before I knock off. "What'll it be?"

He smiles. "How's the fish?"

I lean over the counter and whisper into his ear. "Not off the last boat. Or the one before."

"A toasted English and a cup of coffee, then."

"Oh, Michael. That's no way to eat." I stick a slice of cheese on the muffin after turning it over; the cheese becomes soft and bubbly while he watches. "On the house."

When I'm through, he walks with me back to Porter Square to the trolley stop. No trolleys run at that hour, though; they're all stowed in the car barn. You have to wait for the Arlington bus.

"It surprises me, you working at Lenny's."

"Why?"

"You used to talk about nursing in a mental hospital." I must have said that in Charlie's room; I don't even remember.

"I couldn't cope with that now."

He looks perplexed.

"I could make beds, sure. Rows and rows of clean white beds, tight draw sheets, spreads smooth and pillows in fat stacks."

It's cold, standing at the trolley stop. Michael wraps his scarf twice around his throat.

"You don't have to wait with me. I'm okay."

"You still haven't explained."

"I can't deal with people any more. They make such a mess of things. Bleeding into their bedding and demanding things and covering bedside tables with candy boxes. I wouldn't be able to . . . control them." I laugh to break the tension. "Besides, there are plenty of crazies at Lenny's."

"Then why do you work at all?"

"I have to get out."

"Pat hates it, you know."

"Does he? He doesn't tell me."

"Maureen ..."

"Here's the bus. 'Night, Michael. Thanks."

Over the Porter Square shopping center alternating candles and Santa Clauses embellish the roofs. There are wreath needles and exhaust stains embedded in the piles of snow, plowed and glazed over, at the outer edges of the parking lot. Angela rides on my hip like a small red monkey in her snowsuit. We've bought wrapping paper and ornaments for our tree.

In the shoe store boots are on sale, ankle-length rubber galoshes, not the puckered vinyl pull-ons that are fashionable this year; they'll move at the regular price until Washington's Birthday.

We stop in, but only Gowan is there. "Pat's gone out for coffee. Is there some way I can help you, Maureen?" He chooses a balloon from behind the counter for Angela, stretches it between his hands and blows it up, his cheeks puffed out like a hamster's. He has a lot of wind power— from the singing, I suppose. He ties the neck of the balloon with a length of shoe-box cord and presents it to Angela.

He says again, "Something I can do for you, Maureen?"

"No, just tell Pat I said hello."

Walking by the hairdresser's, I notice a girl standing in the doorway, smoking a cigarette. In spite of the cold, she is wearing only a white nylon uniform. She grins at me, and I realize there's something familiar about her. The hair is now orange and she's put on some weight, but there's no doubt about it. Lorna.

26

Gowan comes to Lenny's nearly every night now. He drinks his coffee leaning against the carry-out counter, watching me finish up.

Scrubbing the steam table, I say, "Don't wait for me tonight, Michael. Mary didn't come in, so I have to wash the dishes from the grill before I can go."

"I'll help you."

"You're not in the union."

"If the Amalgamated Dishwashers find me and break all my knuckles, I'll sing for a living. People will drop coins into my hat and pat me gently on the head. 'Poor fellow, what a noble sacrifice,' they'll say."

"Right in the middle of Porter Square."

"Of course."

"You don't own a hat."

"I do. It belonged to my mother. Tastefully decorated with cherries it is, too."

"Michael Gowan, you are touched in the head."

He ducks under the counter, drops his coat and scarf on a chair and takes over the sink. "Did you hear about the Irishman who burned his neck ironing his shirt? Did you hear about the Irishwoman who fell out the window ironing her curtains?" He's up to his elbows in soap.

I give the cups a shake and stack them on the shelf over the stove to dry. "Shut up, Michael," but I'm laughing.

"Okay." He sings, "For I met her in the garden where the praties grow." Chorus after chorus.

"Michael, what are praties?"

"How should I know? What do you think I am, Irish? Only Poles tell Irish jokes."

"All right, Pole. Here's your coat; let's go."

We walk across the empty Porter Square parking lot, over to Massachusetts Avenue. It's raining a little, "spitting," Michael calls it, and the Arlington bus is slow in coming. Michael's head is just at the same level as my own.

"Pat will be worrying about you," he says, refolding his scarf around his neck against the chill.

"He never worries about anything."

"Be serious, Maureen."

"I am serious. I promise you he's in bed asleep by now."

"Maureen. I'm an Irish joke myself, walking backwards in a minefield swinging a mine detector."

"What are you talking about?"

He doesn't answer.

After work I look for his house on Arcadia Street. It's a small wooden house, painted yellow, with bare wistaria branches wrapped around the porch railing like twine. He's put a Christmas wreath on the door.

He lifts his hands helplessly when he answers my ring. We stand together in the entryway. "You've found me out, Maureen."

"Pat said you have the flu. I suppose he got it wrong, as usual."

"No, that's what I told him, but it wasn't the truth." He looks worried and sad. He's in his shirt sleeves, with his trousers too big and puckered around his middle by his belt.

Perhaps, I think, he didn't want to see me any more. It's an odd, dismal feeling.

"Every now and then I get totally fed up with feet," he says. "I have such a dread of going to the store I can't make myself." He smiles and rearranges the stray hairs on top of his bald spot.

"Well, here I stand like an idiot, holding a quart of Lenny's chowder." The soup has sloshed out of the cardboard container and is dripping into my fingers.

"I'm the idiot."

"I'm just glad you're all right. I'll go now."

"I haven't eaten, actually. If you looked in my icebox, you'd find half a jar of olives and a can of tobacco."

"Tobacco?"

"So it won't dry out, but I always forget to fill my pouch."

There's a sudden squawk from inside. "The parrot?"

"Yes, the nosy beast. Look, Maureen, come in and share some chowder with me." The urgency in his voice is surprising. "Or . . . maybe you think it wouldn't be appropriate."

"We must be beyond needing a chaperone by now."

"We old people."

"Yes."

In the kitchen, he sets the soup carton on the table and cleans my hands with a towel. He's embarrassed by the intimacy. He drops the towel and turns away from me, pours the soup into a saucepan and lights the electric ring under it. More curious squawks emerge from another part of the house, but he doesn't pay any attention.

"Do you feel old, Maureen?"

"I sometimes think I was never young at all."

"But I don't know enough to be old."

"Yes, that too."

His kitchen is neat, clearly unchanged from his mother's time. Ruffled curtains over the kitchen sink, a checked tablecloth on the table. When the soup is hot, he ladles it into shallow bone-china bowls. "The only two left that aren't chipped," he admits.

We are very quiet; there's only the sound of spoons ringing on china. He's in a strange mood. It's not like him not to have a lot to say. "Was it your idea to come?" he asks finally.

"Pat told me to stop in after work and find out whether you needed anything. Once in a while he thinks about someone besides himself, but then he usually makes a botch of it."

"You're not fair to him."

"I'm always maneuvering you between us, aren't I? I'm sorry; it's awkward for you."

"Maureen, I care what happens to you. It doesn't have anything to do with Pat."

Our bowls are empty. Abruptly he picks them up and rinses them under the tap.

"Thank you for telling me that."

He shrugs. "I can't help it."

No help for it. A long time passes while he stands at the sink, letting the tap water trickle through his fingers. I feel, then, how much I'd like to lie next to him on his bed and be caressed—gently, gently—in every part, by those clever fingers. Not needing to think about anything, not caring what I'd be falling into.

"I'm hanging on," I say, in a low troubled voice.

He turns. "Are you talking about Pat? About hanging onto him?"

"I suppose I am. I owe him a lot, Michael."

"You owe something to yourself."

"More to him, though." Once on this tack, I have to stick with it. I only half believe it myself, but no doubt Michael will readily accept my loyalty to Pat. Kind men are easily gulled.

I get up from the table, straighten the checked cloth. He lays his hand on my arm.

"Before you go, I want to show you something."

He leads me into the room that had once been his mother's. It is completely empty—no bed, chairs, curtains. His hand is still on my arm, trembling. He is so open to me that I can almost see his emotions pulsating, like the heart in a dissected chick embryo. When have I ever been like that, except with Charlie? And that so long ago, it seems, that I can hardly remember what it was like.

He opens his mother's closet door, and there are all her clothes, still hanging there. Shoes in tidy pairs on the floor; on the shelf the hat with cherries I'd thought was apocryphal. "I've never been able to give them away."

"Do you want me to do it for you?" It would be terrible, though, folding into boxes all those sagging dresses which smell of lilac cachet and have armholes permanently stained.

"Yes, sometime," he says vaguely. Obviously, I haven't caught his meaning. "That was the reason."

"For what?"

"That I have never married. I kept thinking of Mother's clothes, hanging in there."

"But why are you telling me?"

"You wouldn't have wanted to take her place."

"If I loved you, I suppose I would have."

"And if I loved you, I would have wanted you to. That's a paradox, isn't it?"

We are each silent, thinking about the implications of what we've said. Luckily, it is all very conditional, impersonal. The moment of tension has already passed.

"It wouldn't have been possible anyway for me to take her place."

"No."

I button up my coat. "Good night, Michael."

"Shall I walk you to the bus?"

"No, not tonight."

"All right. Good night, Maureen," he says lightly.

27

I see Charlie's wife walking along Rindge Avenue carrying a bunch of orange gladioli wrapped in plastic. She walks in small pinched steps. She must be going to visit his grave. I am jealous of her. I am passionate in my grief. Uncle Frank was wrong about me.

I've had to quit work, because I can't leave Angela with Gran any more. My grandmother's mind is beginning to go. A series of tiny strokes, the doctor thinks, bleeding into her brain and confusing her, but not doing enough damage to cause paralysis. Her arthritis is bad, too. Angela is willful and surprisingly strong, walking now, too much of a handful for Gran.

"Come stay with Pat and me. We'll find a bigger place."

"I won't leave my home, and that's that."

She'll be seventy-seven on her next birthday. I guess

she just wore out after raising two generations. Stiff gray whiskers are growing on her chin. "I moved my bowels this morning," she tells me, as triumphantly as though she'd delivered a baby. She hides things so they won't be stolen. She keeps rolled-up crumpled dollar bills in the icebox and her treasures, mostly worthless, in little jars and boxes secreted all over the house. Sometimes she won't let Pat's mother in the door, communicates with her in the space the chain lock leaves. Yet she invites the delivery boy from the drugstore in for cake and tea and leaves him alone in the kitchen, up to God knows what, while she stumbles to the bathroom on her bad legs and then starts to think about something else and forgets all about him.

She says to me, "You have a good head and a good heart below it, and that's all you need in this world, God love you." Probably echoing something her own mother said long ago. Well, I could use a little money, too. I miss Lenny's pay check and the feeling of independence it meant.

Gran's fingering her old black-beaded rosary. "I took care of people all my life, and I don't ask for a thing. I don't want to trouble nobody. I just trust to God."

"But Pat and I like to help you. Do you think we don't?"

"I didn't say that, did I?" She scrubs at the table with a rag, trying to erase the teacup rings that have been there since I was a child. "God has a program. Everybody fighting and quarreling, knocking each other over the head, that's how He means to end the world. Maybe not tomorrow. But if you think this old world's going to go on forever, you're wrong."

It's like her to decide to take it with her when she goes, I think, smiling to myself, but I feel a sharp tight knot in the back of my neck when I'm putting away her groceries. All that talk about God all of a sudden, it's scary. The state of her bowels and God, that's all she thinks about now.

Sometimes she calls Angela "Maureen." And sometimes when she's fondling the child, I think it's her own Angie she's remembering.

Last week I gave her money to pay the paper boy, but instead she went to the five-and-dime in Harvard Square, struggling all that way on the trolley, and what she came home with was a glass ashtray, broken because she dropped the package on the sidewalk.

"What did you need it for anyway, Gran? You don't even smoke."

She thought about it for a long time. "I must have bought it for Pat." She began to weep over the broken pieces. "It was a present for him, and now look at it. Oh, the poor man."

I have now a pair of faint creases on each side of my mouth, like paper folded by mistake and then ironed out. I am only twenty-three. I suppose I am one of those people who goes directly from looking twelve to looking forty without any in-between. Also, I have been letting my hair grow, but I don't think it's a success. The dark wisps don't conform very well to the shape of my head, they drag untidily across the shoulders of my polo shirt. I can't even look at myself in the mirror without Angela pulling at my legs to be picked up or whimpering in another room over a lost toy.

Pat's drinking whiskey now instead of beer.

It is a freak hot day in early spring, and Cissy and I arrange a picnic with husbands and children. Sunday. We sit under the evergreens at Fresh Pond, eating salami sandwiches and hard-boiled eggs. The children crunch egg shells into the grass.

Vince takes snapshots. We are forever immortalized. Me with my round bland face, repacking a lunch bag; the toddlers trailing rubber pants; Cissy crossing her legs at just the right angle to make them look slimmest; Pat dragging on a cigarette. Vignettes of family life.

Extracting the roll from the camera, Vince says, "We're thinking of moving back up to your part of town."

"We saw a real nice apartment. Three bedrooms." Cissy is pinning a diaper on Reba, who is struggling to get away. "We'll need a bigger place soon," she says meaningfully.

All of us get sunburned. When Pat and I are home he says, "God, they breed like rabbits." His high forehead is flushed with booze and sun.

"Does that bother you?"

"No, it doesn't bother me."

"Pat, I wish . . ."

"What?"

"I don't know." I don't know. I wish I could have Pat's baby and forget about Charlie and forget about the longing and hunger always picking away at me. And at the same time I want nothing to do with anybody alive. I'm mad as a hatter, crazy as a loon.

I pinch away the new leaves on my geranium to make it bushy. The pale-green leaves are in my palm, coarse-smelling, crumpled.

"Your grandmother's failing, isn't she? My mother says so."

"She's a tough old bird. She's got a bit of life in her yet."

The traffic rumbles along Rindge Avenue. It's hard to talk. There's so little of my family left. Even though the smell of spring is in the air, I don't think about anything but dying.

Pat breaks the seal on a new whiskey bottle. I cook supper for him, but I go to bed alone.

Cissy is pregnant again, up the pole again. Her new apartment is in the brick housing compound on Rindge Avenue. The day she moves in is Ash Wednesday, buds on the stunted crabapple trees in the courtyard. Late afternoon, sun hitting the windows, graffiti on the brick walls. Not obscenities, just names inscribed with chalk: Steve, Mike, Ella.

She's getting all set up, separating her utensils into plastic compartments in the dull back kitchen. It overlooks the railway track, and I envy her that connection with movement, but it's only a nuisance to her, the noise of the trains on their way in and out of Boston.

"They'll run out of money, shut the railroad down, Maureen. From what I read in the papers, it's only a question of time."

I want to say: What happens then, Cissy? Will your life be happier then, will there be picnic grounds in the railway bed? We're unwrapping plates and cups from newspaper and arranging them on her new shelves. Her belly is swollen and her back aches, but she's used to it by now. There's a smudge of ash between her eyes.

The children are playing in the packing boxes; one box tips over and a child cries. It doesn't matter which child. We comfort them absently and drink our coffee. "Vince got a raise last week."

"That's great, Cissy."

"Oh, you don't notice the difference. You still can't pay all the bills."

*   *   *

"The chicken's not done. There's blood in the joints."

"I'm sorry, Pat."

He pushes the plate away. "I hate chicken anyway."

"You never said that before."

"You don't listen to what I say."

He unscrews the cap from the whiskey bottle and puts the neck to his mouth. I scrape the plates into the garbage pail.

"Well, you *don't* listen, Maureen." No doubt he's right. I'm too entangled in my inner thoughts, and whatever he says is meaningless.

He's out back, practicing shots. I happen to see him from the bedroom window. The ball hits the backboard hard; it skims the rim and, by the grace of God, falls inside the hoop. In my imagination he's throwing something else. Stones. We are children and he's aiming stones at the windows of the paper mill. I must have been able to hear glass splintering, but all I remember is the look on his face: dreamy, intent. I watched from the safety of the scrabble of weed trees below the factory, afraid I'd be caught. But Pat didn't mind standing there right out in the open hurling these stones.

He tosses the ball again; he doesn't miss. He is a graceful man in some ways.

28

Peggy sold her car to Pat because she says she's getting too shortsighted to drive. He has to cross wires under the hood to get it started in the morning. I think she should have paid him to take it away, but it's not up to me to interfere between them. They rattle at each other enough as it is. Pat and me not going to Mass. Peggy smoking too much. Pat forgetting to clip her hedge. And so on. It actually takes him longer to get to work driving the thing than it did when he rode the trolley. I'm glad to see that fat ungainly Chevy parked in the driveway, though. You kick it, just like you give the television set a sharp smack on the side to get it to focus or you beat on the icebox to make it stop rumbling. Good basic American technology. Old appliances are like old friends.

"Let's plant a garden this year, Pat. Vegetables."

Grumbling, he's out in the back yard turning over the sod, picking out rocks and pieces of broken glass and cinder, raking manure in. He brings me a fragment of blue-and-white pottery that he found in the dirt. I can tell it's willow pattern, like the teapot I gave Charlie. I rinse it off and leave it on the windowsill in the kitchen where I can see it while I'm washing dishes. Perhaps, if Pat notices it there, he thinks I treasure it as a token of love from him. It could be that I do.

We have sugar peas, climbing raggedly up a string net, and then lettuce in pale, delicate bunches like wrinkled tissue paper.

In July the tomato plants have tough green fruit hidden in their branches. They give off a sweaty smell when I work among them, snapping off their bottom suckers and tying them to stakes. Mr. Boyle from next door leans over the fence and tells me not to work in the beans when they are wet; the blossoms will fall off and mold will spread from leaf to leaf.

Uncle Frank calls it my Victory Garden. I can see why; gardening is a series of battles. Me pitted against aphids, slugs, white fly, cut-worms, leaf mold. I think the bugs are going to win. They are so fecund.

In the evening I soak the garden with the hose and the baby toddles into the spray, laughing. Pat lies in the grass, sipping from a beer can, batting away the gnats. He's only good for the heavy work, he says; anything that takes brains is for the women in the family. I give him a squirt from the hose; he grabs it from me and douses me in return. The neighbors are watching from their windows. We have a good time together when we play like children. The trouble is we aren't children any more.

Cissy and I are in the supermarket pushing our baskets along the aisle. The little girls sit up front in the baskets, dangling their legs, and Ronny trails behind, whining for cereals and candy bars he's seen advertised on television.

All of a sudden we see Charlie's wife going the wrong way down the one-way aisle. She's touching in a tentative way one can and then another, unable to decide. She doesn't notice us.

Around the corner, Cissy whispers to me, "You know who that was, don't you? Charlie O'Clair's wife. You know what I heard? She gave out apples with razor blades in them last Halloween."

"Oh, Cissy, why do you listen to gossip like that?"

"Everybody says she's crazy. It's common knowledge."

"Common, all right." I'm putting a sack of onions into my cart and wondering if I have enough money to buy nectarines.

Across the aisle from the produce, Cissy chooses a package of hair coloring. She has to touch up her roots. "You know, I feel sorry for her. Poor frustrated old witch."

Cissy's belly is round and low; her smock is faded; it's the third time around for it, maybe more. Probably she inherited it from one of her sisters.

"Why frustrated? Because she has no children?"

Cissy laughs. "Maureen, you can be so stupid."

Saturday. The garbage needs to be taken out, the laundry is piling up, the electricity bill is lost—fallen behind the radiator, or somewhere. By extension everything seems crumbling, unsteady under the foot. This is the hottest summer in living memory.

When I cross my index and middle fingers and put them to my lips, I can't tell which finger is which. Pat tunes the radio in to progressive jazz, music to have a nervous breakdown by. Shall I cut my hair? I pick up the scissors and am blocked by indecision.

There are infant aphids deposited on every leaf in my garden. If I spray, I poison. But I couldn't possibly pick them all off one by one and drop them into kerosene; there's not that much time in a summer. It's so hot in this attic apartment the sweat sticks my shirt to my back and trickles down behind my knees. I guess we'll have eggs for supper. Hard-boiled and sliced. Bread and butter. Maybe green tomatoes in bread-crumb batter, fried in a pan.

The telephone rings and Pat takes it. "Gowan wants to know if we can go to the movies tonight. He says there's a good show on at the Brattle."

I'd like to sit next to my friend Michael in a chilled theater, my bare arm sometimes touching the sleeve of his jacket. I'd like it too much.

"I can't leave Angela with Gran any more, you know that."

"What about my mother?"

"I don't feel like asking her."

"Jesus, Maureen."

I hear him telling Gowan that I won't go but that he'll meet him later. White seeds spill out of the tomatoes. I try to be a good and faithful wife. In one way or another, I always fail.

I've been to the dentist and I hurry across the parking lot, hoping to catch a ride home with Pat. My tooth throbs and the filling is uneven. I never have novocain. The dentist said the filling will wear down in my mouth and I'll stop noticing it. My gums are receding, he said. Unusual in a person my age. What were my parents' teeth like? When I said I didn't know, his look was curious but as cool and sweet as his mouthwash. I'm going to have big trouble with my gums one of these days. No need to worry yet, though.

Angela is a crank, hungry and weary with being passed from one dental assistant to another while my mouth was jacked open. Good luck, though. The Chevy's still in the parking lot in front of the shoe store.

Gowan takes out a red balloon and pulls it back and forth like an accordion. Angela grabs for it before he's even blown it up.

"What do you mean, Pat's gone? The car's right out front."

I can see that he's stalling with the balloon, groping for some lie. All at once it strikes me.

"Where are they? In the back?"

Miserably, he shakes his head. They must do it in the hairdressing shop, then. I imagine Pat and Lorna coupling on the floor in the midst of curl papers and snips of hair.

"It wasn't his fault, Maureen. She kept hanging around."

"I suppose he was about as hard to catch as an eel in a bucket."

"Eel." Angela likes the word. She tries it out again on her tongue. "Eel."

"Never mind, Michael. We'll take the trolley."

It's only what I deserve, after all.

29

The summer ends. The garden is dug up and composted; the days grow short and when the sun shines it is pale and low in the sky. I am reminded of the first months of my marriage, when we first came to Winter Street. In retrospect the time seems perfectly calm and happy, the sun shining in the kitchen window, the long Sunday afternoons, incredibly drawn out and amber, like pulled molasses taffy. If there were any dark and discordant aspects of those days, I don't remember them. In fact, I can't put my finger on what went wrong.

The two years of our marriage are just gone, I don't know where. The mind is an odd thing: how it fails to recognize things that are shifting and changing, fails to hang onto those bits and pieces of living. What was Angela like when she was newborn? I can't remember, except by looking at the snapshots Pat took, and because he developed them himself, they are fading and brownish. The scene, a girl bathing an infant on the kitchen table, is like the view through the bottom of a drinking glass, queerly contracted and distorted.

Surely that smiling gawky girl is not me. At what imperceptible point did I stop being young, with nothing but possibilities before me? Where's the luck Charlie saw in my hand?

Angela unborn was a mystery. But now everything is all laid out. Losing her baby teeth, learning her catechism, making her first Communion, discovering the Brothers Grimm, putting on a wedding veil. Me all over again. And the old me is lost.

Pat is drinking at the kitchen table while I do the washing-up. He comes behind me and puts one hand on each of my breasts. "What are you thinking about, so quiet?"

"Nothing. I'm not thinking about a thing."

He swears and presses a loose edge of linoleum down with his foot.

"Why don't you ever glue it, Pat?"

"Why don't you ever stop nagging at me?" He takes a pint container of ice cream out of the refrigerator and eats directly out of it with a table spoon. Cherry-vanilla. "Cissy should be popping, shouldn't she?"

"Any day."

"Poor Vince. What a rat race."

The tide is like pig-swill: full of seaweed, straw, desiccated oranges. Foaming as though fermenting. The air is chill. Gowan bullies us down to the South Shore on a cloudy Sunday afternoon, I don't know why, some backhanded plot or subtle kind of torture.

Pat carries Angela to the sea edge and swings her over the water so that her bare feet are splashed. Gowan and I, sitting on the concrete steps, can hear her screeches, half delighted, half terrified.

"Where do the oranges come from, Michael?"

"Off ships."

Gowan is trying to light his pipe in the wind and the match keeps going out.

"But how do they get overboard?"

"They fall off, I guess. Maybe the sailors play croquet with them on the deck."

"And what do they use for mallets?"

"Lifeboat oars."

We both laugh quietly. The concrete step is cold and damp, even through my corduroy coat.

"I don't play games much. That's Pat's department."

"Maureen, he doesn't really care about that hairdresser, you know."

"He doesn't care about anything."

Angela presents me with her find: a shell, half of a razor clam. The day is not a success. Nobody can think of anything to say; even Gowan has run out of jokes.

I can't forgive Pat for selling Charlie's watch.

The Buick backs carefully out of the driveway onto Massachusetts Avenue; the woman driving is so short in the seat that one can only see her professionally curled hair and her vague, clouded expression. She goes out every afternoon at one o'clock; I know, because I have begun to keep a close watch on the house. I know, for example, that her gardener comes on Tuesdays to cut the hedge and rake leaves and that a case of sherry is delivered twice a month. That's roughly a bottle a day. I also know that she does her own cooking now and that the groceries are delivered from Sage's in Harvard Square. She takes two newspapers, but often the mailman goes by the house without leaving anything. She must spend her mornings on the telephone, talking to her grocers and wine merchants.

But where does she go in the afternoons? Perhaps she

has a lover. The idea is so insane that I laugh out loud, and Angela laughs too. Although we are standing right on the curb when she drives slowly past, she never seems to recognize me. This, when I think about it, is not surprising. All my life there has been this peculiar thing about me: dogs paw me and people bump into me, not because I am conspicuous but because I am invisible. Either she will run me down in her car, quite unwittingly, or she will continue to pass me every day on her way—where?

Only Charlie ever saw inside me. My longing for him is as sharp and clinging as a barnacle.

The house is in fine shape, recently repainted and the gardens all in order. Does she spend her afternoons running away from memories of him? Or does she not think of him at all? I can't decide which is worse.

From the sidewalk I see the playhouse, visible now that the orchard is pruned and the high grass mowed. Children don't seem to go there any more. Maybe she chases them away. Maybe they'd rather watch television.

"Like they say, don't get mad, get even." Peggy removes her sweater and reveals her sleeveless arms, the flesh on the upper arms puckered, the veins in her wrists like winding dark worms under her skin. For some reason I am reminded of the way Pat used to taunt me, "Worm." She's telling me about trash cans. Some dispute with a neighbor whose dog knocks down Peggy's cans and scatters litter all over the lawn. Peggy got even by hiding behind a bush and squirting the dog with a water pistol filled with ink. Only Peggy could actually execute such a scheme. "Apricot poodle, show dog." She laughs. "Now they'll have to call it plum poodle."

She's brought candy for Angela, and she takes a piece. "Cissy had her baby, I hear."

"Another boy."

"That's nice. Maybe you'll be having one soon."

"I don't know."

"You're not using something, Maureen?"

"No."

"I'll light a candle."

I turn and watch the coffee burbling into the perco-lator top. Not ready yet. Peggy likes her coffee strong and stiff with sugar. Then she smokes to calm her nerves and takes a diet pill.

"Pat would love to have a son. He doesn't talk about it much, but I can tell."

"I thought he doesn't care for the way Cissy and Vince spawn."

"It's different if it's your own kid." She's being motherly, though I know she finds my lack of savvy exas-perating and resents my stubbornness. "Every man wants a son. It's only natural."

Before I say anything, I pour her coffee and hand her the sugar bowl. "Maybe his friend Lorna will give him one."

Her mouth is open; there's a bit of caramel stuck be-tween her lower front teeth.

"Didn't you know, Peggy? He's having an affair with her."

"Are you sure?"

"Yes."

"Don't you worry, I'll put an end to that."

"Some things don't end."

"Oh, you're wrong. Everything ends, sooner or later."

She drinks her coffee, ignoring me, plotting some way to get even with Lorna. I feel like a bystander, curi-ous but uninvolved.

30

Strange tunnels have appeared on the lawn in front of Charlie's house. Do moles burrow in the winter? It is a mystery. Anyway, it amuses me to think how cross she will be when she looks out the window and sees her neat brown lawn all in upheaval. Pat seems to have stopped seeing Lorna. Peggy says something oblique about a bargain struck between her and Pat. That is another mystery.

Christmas coming up again. Our tree this year is actually two spindly trees tied together, each one so uneven it couldn't be sold on its own. When Pat drags the tree into the front room and I point this out to him, at first he's irritated and then he laughs. "Two for the price of one." Untangling the strings of bulbs, he says, "We'll have two angels, one for each treetop." Nothing ever bothers him for long.

Elaine Ford

This will have to be Gran's last Christmas on Verdun Street. She's so confused now that Peggy is worried
about getting the fire insurance renewed, never mind
about burning up in her own bed. I guess I'll have to find
a bigger apartment, cough up the extra money some way,
force her to move in with us. I dread the thought, not of
caring for her but of cleaning out her old place—all the
junk she's stored away for over twenty years. She'll fight
like a cat over each chipped plate and rhinestone pin. The
funny thing is, she doesn't have memories to connect with
the junk; she got it all at Gilchrist's or Kresge's. She's had
to decorate her whole inner life with cheap goods bought
in bargain stores. Peggy said, "Well, let her have one more
Christmas at home." Peggy has a kind face, in spite of her
two husbands and thousands of schemes. I can see her
leaping out from behind a bush at Lorna and covering her
in ink, but it would all be in the spirit of good clean re-
venge. She'd never hold a grudge.

Angela helps me hang the ornaments on the tree. Her
fingers are small but not clumsy, not peasant's hands like
mine. She likes the silver and gold balls best. She was
born, I think, to live in that big house with the damask-
covered furniture and the blood-red Persian carpet. Con-
ceived there, she belongs to it more than somebody who
just unpacked a suitcase and moved in. Certainly more
than that squat woman whose father was a building con-
tractor from South Boston and well known for making
deals smelling worse than Boston Harbor.

I hug Angela and she squirms away from me, grabbing for the box of ornament hooks. She is not yet two,
but somehow I know she'll have the same struggles as I,
always craving something she can't quite reach.

We haven't had snow yet this year. Everyone seems
on edge, waiting for something: the gas man who comes to

178

read the meter, the shop girl who sells me an extension cord, the clerk in the post office, Gran. The clouds are low and pregnant, but no snow falls. It's not Christmas without snow, everyone says. I go alone to Midnight Mass and walk back on the bare pavements, up Rindge Avenue to the traffic light, right on Montgomery, three blocks down to Winter Street. I can see the Christmas tree in our front room on the top floor, the bulbs lit. But when I unlock the door I find that Pat is asleep and the radio in the kitchen is playing carols in ragtime. I begin to cry. I don't know why; I haven't cried in years.

New Year's Eve. There is a moon, faint as though wrapped in gauze, and a tentative snow skittering in the air. Jokers are in the streets, beating on stop signs and gates, cracking bottles in the gutter, singing off-key. It's still early, though, not yet nine.

"We'll go over to Gowan's and have a drink with him," Pat says. He's been drinking already—for his sore throat, he says—and sucking horehound drops so that he smells medicinal. His nose is red.

"Maybe he has a date."

"Are you kidding? Get dressed, and I'll take Angela over to my mother's."

"She's asleep."

"So? She can go to sleep again."

I lift the small body out of her crib and button her coat over her pajamas. Her head flops against my shoulder as though she is a stuffed doll. I hold her in my arms a moment, unwilling to hand her over to him.

"You'll make your cold worse going out."

"You don't care about that, do you? You just don't want to go."

I don't say anything; I am feeling the gentle rise and

fall of Angela's chest against mine, listening to her heartbeat.

"Is it my friends you don't like? Or me?"

There's no answer to that, not even a lame one. He's right: I am hard, unloving, stiff with impossible desires. I hear him go down the back stairs, carrying the baby, and I resolve to be a good wife. I shall cut my brain entirely off.

I go to the closet and find the silk and gold-threaded dress that Pat bought for me. It is out of shape and creased, hanging so long unworn. I put it on in the dark so that I can't see my own pallor exposed by it.

He is gone a very long time. The tree lights blink on and off, on and off; finally I unplug the cord. Very faintly, I hear St. John's striking eleven. Perhaps Pat misunderstood our last words and drove over to Gowan's without me. Surely he did not crash. The police come around in pairs and break it to you when they've found cars with wrenched body structures and people with broken spines. I pick up the phone and dial Gowan's number.

"No, Maureen, he's not here."

The same thought hits both of us. Lorna.

"Look, Maureen, I'll come over."

"No, Michael. It doesn't matter." I hang up without waiting for his answer. Shall I call Peggy? No. I'm sure Angela is sleeping peacefully in Pat's old bed. He's always very careful with her, no matter what else he does.

As I unhook the back of the ugly black dress, I look outside and see that it is snowing harder. No more moon. A white covering on the roads, crisscrossed by tire marks at the corner of Winter and Montgomery. Snowflakes swirling, flinging themselves back into the sky in the light of the street lamp. I pull on my nightgown and lie between cold sheets. I'm waiting to hear the church bells strike twelve, but I doze off and miss it.

*   *   *

A bell ringing insistently. Fire? No smell of smoke.
Pat must be at the door, lost his key, drunk.

But it is Gowan standing there in the doorway. "I
walked." Snow has crystallized to the strands of his hair.
"I couldn't get a taxi. Buses aren't running."

His coat is soaked. From underneath it he takes a holiday-wrapped box of whiskey. There are sad little puckers
in the red and gold striped paper.

"You are frozen, you madman." I take his coat to the
kitchen and drape it over the radiator. The arms hang
down, defeated. He's watching me moving in my nightgown. My hair is all awry.

"It's turned into a proper storm, a blizzard."

"You shouldn't have come."

"Well, once you start . . ." He's shivering.

"Shall we open it?"

He looks at the whiskey box, surprised that he's carried it all this way. "Pat's not home?"

"No."

I put two glasses on the coffee table in the front
room. We sit next to each other on the sofa. We are old
friends. He strips the box from the bottle and unscrews
the cap. We drink the whiskey neat. It is coarse in our
throats, a counterirritant.

He has no joke; he does not even wish me compli-
ments of the season. We sit quietly, side by side. The
room looks bare, every corner exposed by the pole lamp.
The wicker in the basket chair is ragged in the bottom,
about to fall through, probably. The floor underneath our
ungainly double-angled tree is sprinkled with dry needles.
A few opened gifts are there: the pink slippers Pat gave
me, the yellow pullover I gave Pat, still displayed in their
store boxes. A draft through the closed window flutters

181

the white curtains. I have never sewed the hem in two years.

Suddenly a third of the bottle is gone. I am hungry for it, in a way I have never been before. Gowan too is drinking steadily. I want to touch him, comfort him.

"Did you know I loved Charlie O'Clair?"

"I guessed it."

"What else did you know?"

He looks at me, not shy any more, but waiting for me to talk.

Instead, without knowing why, I begin to unbutton the top of my nightgown. This time, he doesn't look away. His face is very close to me. I lift my left breast toward his mouth. He sucks hard, greedily. Charlie used to do that. I had no milk then; I have no milk now.

I reach down between his legs.

"Oh, Maureen."

"It's all right, it's all right."

He sleeps on the sofa and is up before dawn, tramping away over the soft snow; I don't even hear him leave. When I wake the apartment is empty, his coat gone from the radiator, the glasses rinsed and put away, the whiskey bottle poked down into the bottom of the trash can.

Charlie my lover, Michael my friend.

I look in the mirror. I would not be surprised to find no reflection there at all.

31

Snow is so heavy on the trees the branches crackle. Rindge Avenue is always plowed so that the fire engines can get through to the public housing—the incinerators are forever catching fire—but all the side streets are clogged. Cars buried, not to be dug out until spring. I am hoping, stupidly, that I can get to Peggy's house before Angela soaks the mattress. She was wearing no diaper when Pat took her away, and Peggy would not think to get her up at night to use the toilet. The snow is higher than the tops of my boots. If you have cold feet you don't have to worry about anything important. There are some blessings God dumps on us.

No life in Peggy's apartment, but I don't panic, because I can hear voices upstairs. I find the three of them sitting at the kitchen table having tea and toast. This must be one of Gran's good days. She is presiding over the teapot and cutting Angela's toast into neat buttered triangles. Yet I think she hardly recognizes me.

"She didn't wet the bed, did she?"

Peggy smiles. "Dry as a bone, the little lamb. How was the party?"

Party. It seems so long ago that we planned to go to Gowan's I can scarcely answer. "Fine," I say vaguely.

She laughs, spreading jam on her toast. "Hung, are you? In the old days we had parties like that, grand wild affairs. I guess Pat's still in bed."

I don't tell her what bed Pat's in. He'll turn up eventually, no point in getting her all excited. I pour myself a cup of tea, but for some reason I don't like the taste any more.

"Shall we go home?" I ask my daughter.

"Feet," Gran says.

Her mind has focused on the thing I've forgotten; I can't carry Angela home in the snow without something on her feet. I brought no socks or shoes for her.

Gran heaves herself out of her chair and reaches for the pair of cotton stockings that are hanging to dry over the stove. Nothing seems incongruous any more. I pull the long fat stockings up Angela's legs, folding over the tops so they reach back down to her toes. They are pink; they smell of bacon; they are warm. Again, I feel like crying. My mother never knew my baby, and when I come to think about it, I don't know her either.

"I'll have to call that Gallagher about getting the street plowed," Gran says. We all know it's hopeless, though, we have no influence; it's just something you say, like making violent threats to blow up the gas company.

"All's well that ends," Peggy says, helping herself to another piece of toast. She's had a funny education; we all have. But maybe not so bad. We pull through.

Pat's still not home when Angela and I unlock the back door and fiddle with the thermostat to get the radiators working. I plug in the tree and set it blinking to amuse Angela, and then I pick Pat's shirts out of the tangle in the laundry basket. They have to be sprinkled, rolled up neck inside neck, left to dampen while the iron heats on the board.

I lick my finger and touch it to the iron to see if it's hot enough. St. John's is ringing, ringing, calling the flock to Mass on New Year's Day.

And then there's a great noise coming up the back stairs: Cissy and her three children. "The snow," they say, shaking their boots all over the kitchen floor and leaving their coats and snowsuits everywhere. "A grand snow, Maureen. I've been teaching the children how to make angels. Remember we used to do that? Lying on our backs in the snow and moving our arms, and when you get up it's like angels with wings there in the snow. I could never get over that. I mean it was only you and me but we left angels there."

"Dogs pissed in them."

"Oh, for Christ's sake, Maureen."

I put milk on to boil and stir cocoa powder in. I need another saucepan to warm the baby's bottle. I strike the match and the gas makes a minuscule explosion. Call the landlady. A fat lot of good that will do.

"Where's Pat?"

Shall I tell her that I don't know, that maybe I'll never see him again?

"Out."

"So's Vince. Playing hockey. I don't know how, tons of snow all over the ice. They'll have to shovel it off." She extracts a cigarette from her handbag and looks around for an ashtray. I don't bother to help her; if the milk boils over the whole stove has to taken apart and cleaned. She settles on a saucer from the dish drainer. She squirts milk from the baby's bottle onto her wrist to test it and then plugs the nipple into the kid's mouth. His name is Vincent. He has the same dark drugged look as his father. I foresee decade after decade of new Ranellis. Why not?

The three toddlers are carrying mugs of cocoa, dripping it all over the rag rug in the front room. Luckily it is a rug that doesn't show stains. You can spill anything on it and it becomes part of the pattern and color design, possibly even an improvement.

The tip of the iron is going delicately around the buttons. Then long straight sweeps down the front panels. Baby Vincent slurps away.

One shirt folded, the arms tucked in and the breast flat, the collar stiff with starch. The second one laid out on the board. A button missing. Well, he can hide it with his tie. Maybe I'll get around to sewing it on next time. The collar gets done twice, first at the beginning and then at the end. Why? My grandmother did it that way. You never escape.

"I didn't wish you a happy new year, Maureen."

"Thanks for the wish. You too, Cissy."

Her brows are completely plucked out and penciled in. It must hurt, tweezing them out one by one that way, each hair. We have different perceptions of pain.

"There's something I wanted to tell you for a long time. I didn't have the nerve." Air bubbles are rising into Vincent's bottle.

New Year's is when you're supposed to settle old debts, old scores. What now? I wonder.

The tip of the iron points down to the cuff. All around the sleeve, a sharp crease from shoulder to wrist. The cuffs, the collar. Then folding the arms under and dividing the shirt into thirds. Number-two shirt on the pile.

"I wasn't a virgin when I married."

I expect some saga of fumbling in Vince's car after

football games. That's between Cissy and Vince; what does it have to do with me?

"I was twelve. I went to the playhouse behind Old Man Morris' house. I went with that boy Norman in our class."

I remember Norman. He had a thin rat face and wore knickers, handed down from older brothers, long after all the other boys were in long pants. He had the job of delivering the milk trays to the kindergarten and first-grade classes at eleven every morning. Not because he was trustworthy. The teacher wanted to get rid of him. One year he had ringworm and had to be moved to a special seat with empty seats all around him; otherwise he sat in the front row with the other trouble-makers.

"He said he only wanted to look at me. That's all I was going to do, honest. He said he'd take me to the Carnival if I let him. But then, before I knew what was going on, he did it."

"In the playhouse."

"I never let anybody else touch me again until I married, not even Vince. I swear it, Maureen."

"What difference does it make now?"

She is shocked by my casual lack of concern. I guess she expected me to blow up like the gas works. I'm on the third shirt. "I mean, that one time in the playhouse didn't scar you for life or anything."

The baby, sated, is asleep on her lap. She lights another cigarette. "I was so scared when I went to Confession. I thought Father Terrence was going to have a heart attack when I told him. All he did was cough and give me some Hail Marys to say. He must have heard a lot of stories about the playhouse."

"What do you mean?"

"Well, Maureen, you know. Everyone went there to make out."

I look up from the ironing board and she laughs.

"Didn't you know that?"

"No."

"Maureen, you are so innocent." She collects her children and zips and buttons them back into their snowsuits. "I never got to the Carnival anyway. The bastard."

After she's gone, I think about all those kids screwing in the playhouse. I think about Charlie, too. I get out the old yellowed newspaper clipping and see for the first time that he's standing with his shoulder pressed to the shoulder of a young dark-haired woman, who is not looking at the photographer but at him. I remember also something I heard about his secretary, how she performed more services than they teach at secretarial school. I paid no attention then; I can't even recall who said it.

Nothing is the same any more. An ornament shatters and Angela cries. Brushing the shards into the dust pan, I try to think who I am. I shall cut my hair. I shall go back to the beginning. But where was that? Half rain, half sleet is splintering on the window glass.

"I wasn't where you thought." Pat hasn't slept; his coat is wrinkled and his face unshaven. "I went to find my sister."

"I thought you didn't know who she is."

"My mother told me. In exchange for—well, she told me."

"And?"

"I didn't get there. No buses were leaving on account of the storm, but they don't tell you, they just keep you waiting in line hour after hour."

"Why did you pick that moment? To look for her."

He sits at the kitchen table. There are seven shirts in a pile, neatly ironed and folded.

"I had to find somebody who might care—who the hell I am."

The rebuke is bitter. But I'm too tired to sort anything out.

"Are you hungry?"

I put the pan on the burner to heat and scramble a couple of eggs in a bowl. Bread in the toaster. The eggs curl up in the hot butter; I scrape the spatula under them and turn them over. Pat's hand is resting gently on the pile of shirts. We're all right. So far.

32

We are eating Chinese, from the carry-out on Massachusetts Avenue. Sweet and sour spare-ribs, fried rice, moo chee pork. "Hey, what do you think?" Pat says, discarding a bone. "Gowan's getting married."

I assume this is the preamble to some kind of shaggy-dog story cooked up between them, with a punch line like "People who live in grass houses shouldn't stow thrones."

"No, for real. That girl with a bump on her head, Nina Gallagher. It turns out she's got some money stashed away and they're going to open a shoe store in California. 'Why California?' I asked him. 'I thought everyone goes around in bare feet out there.' "

"Well, why?" Biggest open-air mental institution in the world, California. Three thousand miles away from North Cambridge.

"She's got a cousin or something who's going to sell them some property cheap."

"What will they do without him?"

"At the store? The manager's already hired a guy, right out of high school last June. Poor sap doesn't know what he's getting into."

"I'm surprised Michael didn't say something about it. Before everything was so settled."

"It is kind of funny, considering the way Gowan gabs. He didn't want to listen to a lot of ribbing, I guess."

I'm untying Angela's bib and wiping her mouth. So—Charlie's joke about the rich widow and the chicken farm wasn't so wild after all. Chicken farm, shoe store, what's the difference? I wish he'd told me, given me some hint. I haven't seen him since New Year's Eve. It is now the middle of February.

At night Pat pumps away inside me. I lie on my back with his warm semen in me, and then I get up and let it trickle into the toilet. He's asleep when I get back to bed.

I have a pimple next to my nose on my left cheek. Pat has gotten a raise, because he'll be the salesman in charge now. Lent again. Peggy has probably been lighting a lot of candles. I listen to the church bells striking midnight.

The note comes in a brown envelope with a window in it, the kind used for bills, and my name and address are typed. It is written on a piece of lined paper torn out of a notebook. "Maureen. I wanted to tell you myself, but I couldn't figure out how to do it. I'm not very clever about things like that. I'll miss you. Mick."

Mick. He used that nickname to shrink himself, so that if there was any chance of my caring, it would be shriveled. Because I was the only one who had ever called him Michael, except for his mother.

I tear the letter up, envelope and all, and drop it into the wastebasket.

The big house burns. We hear the sirens screaming, and the whole neighborhood rushes over in a mob to see it go up. I can't help going, though I am only one in a crowd, and the police are pushing us back. Sparks in the cold dark sky. The firemen are hosing down the dry cleaner next door so it won't catch. They break the front door down with axes. I can never figure out why they do that; couldn't they at least try to give a polite pull to the bell wire? Pieces of furniture are flung out of the upstairs windows. One yellow velvet chair I recognize; it came from her room. Where is she?

Somebody behind me says she started the fire herself, but I can't believe it. Not deliberately. She would not burn down Charlie's house. Water from the hoses is running all over the sidewalk and into the street. City water, free. They won't send a bill for it.

In the end, the house is only a framework. "Like a turkey the day after Thanksgiving," somebody says. The hedge has been broken down by the firemen and the crowds. "A sin and a shame. Old Man Morris' house, gone." It is as though Charlie never lived there at all. Walking home, I am aware of a strange singed smell in the air, feather mattresses, I suppose.

"Well, have you had enough thrills?" Pat is finishing the newspaper.

"Will you pour me a glass of whiskey?"

I am not a whiskey drinker, but he gets out the bottle and two glasses without any show of surprise. "What happened to the old girl?"

"I couldn't find out. Everybody tells you a different thing."

"Some people like fires. I never thought they were fun."

"You used to throw stones at buildings."

"That's different," he says after drinking some whiskey and thinking about it. "A stone you aim yourself. A fire—once it starts, it takes off on its own, you don't have any control over it any more. You see what I mean?"

Yes, I am beginning to see what he means. Control has always been a very tenuous thing for me; for him it is as easy as tossing a ball or fitting a shoe.

"Pat, do you mind selling shoes?"

He laughs. "The nice things about shoes is that there are twice as many of them as there are people. At least."

"Michael told me once that sometimes he hates people's feet."

He shrugs. "People need shoes. What's wrong with that?"

I can't serve people simply, the way Pat does. I'm always tangled up in my mother's struggles, my father's death, my own cravings.

"It's funny, Maureen, you hardly ever talk to me. I like it when you do."

"But I don't help."

He pours more drink into our glasses. The color is dark amber. The smell of the singed house is still in my nose, although I am many blocks away and our windows are closed.

"There are all kinds of ways of helping."

Yes, but I am restless, uneasy. Angela whimpers over some dream and I am thinking, incongruously, that tomorrow I must fill out the order blank for next summer's seeds.

*　　*　　*

I cut my hair. I use the dull kitchen scissors and once again I am the young girl who looked at the Sacred Heart while snipping away around jug-ears.

Dark scraps of my hair go into the wastebasket and mix with the torn bits of envelope.

A workman is nailing sheets of plywood to the windows, to keep out vandals, I guess, though it seems that every possession is already on the lawn. Sofas, pictures, barrels of china, uneven stacks of books soaking up the hose water.

"Do you know—is Mrs. O'Clair all right?"

"Not a scratch on her. Lucky. They got her out in time."

"Where is she?"

"Are you a friend, or what?"

"Yes, sort of."

"She's staying at a hotel. Looking for an apartment, though, for her and her daughter."

"Her what?"

He bends down to take another handful of nails out of the paper bag and looks at me, suspicious.

"I thought you was a friend."

"I'm sorry, I didn't hear you right."

He's hammering again, making big hard holes in the window frame.

"You know what she told me? Her husband made her promise she wouldn't bring the kid to this house. Well, now the house is burnt, so she's not held to the promise any more, see? She took the girl out of the bug-house and they're going to live somewhere in Arlington. I think that's where she said."

"What's going to happen to the house?"

"Oh, you can't rebuild it. Nobody has that kind of money these days, and besides, it's zoned for business all around here. I guess they'll tear it down, the whole plot, maybe build an office building and a parking lot, plenty of room behind." So that's where she's been going in the afternoons, to see the retarded daughter stuck away in some institution. And now the girl's sprung. He extracted a lot of promises, Charlie did, both from his wife and from me. She was clever enough to get her way finally. Perhaps she let a match gently lick the curtains in her bedroom. She was braver than I, and I am ashamed.

"Do you know where I can reach her?"

He pulls his cap down over his ears and shakes the nails in his hand. "She didn't leave no forwarding address. I could tell her you were asking about her, if you want."

"All right." I recognize one or two books in the pile on the lawn. Manuals. Even Thucydides was a manual, so far as he was concerned. It seemed exciting and sharp at the time; now I am only saddened.

"On second thought, don't bother. I don't think she'd remember me, after all."

33

March. A fidgety month, warm winds blowing, but scabs of old snowfalls still on the streets. Another wedding. This time I am sitting in the congregation, next to a woman in a flat purple hat. Pat and Gowan are again at the altar, but it is Pat who gropes in his breast pocket for the ring. The bride's hair is parted low on her forehead; her eyes are cast to the floor, without expression. She has six bridesmaids and a page, who keeps getting tangled in her train. Gowan smiles.

Afterward the reception is in a hotel on Garden Street. A big crowd, all Gowan's cronies from the time he was political tear-jerker and envelope-licker, plus Gallagher's clubhouse gang. Miniature hotdogs and meatballs on toothpicks are passed among the guests. Pat's toast to the bride is noncommittal; he doesn't know her very well. I suspect Gowan doesn't either, because of the elaborate, courtly way he speaks to her. No verbal short cuts like—I suddenly realize it—like Pat and I have.

I have never seen Gowan looking so pleased with himself. He smiles and pats his head to make sure the strands of hair are firmly plastered over the bald spot. Somebody says, "So you finally got trapped, you old goat. Gallagher got out the shotgun, did he?" And still Gowan smiles.

"Not much of a wedding," Pat whispers to me. "What it needs is a good riot."

"You could always start throwing meatballs."

"Not my style. Meatball that puny wouldn't even make a crack in a window."

I kiss Gowan, but I don't have a chance to say anything, because so many people are pushing around him. And anyway, what would I say? He and his bride are flying to California from Logan Airport this afternoon, but Gallagher's taking care of all the transporting, so this is probably the last I'll ever see of Mick Gowan.

Walking up Garden Street, I suddenly ask Pat, "What's going to happen to the parrot?"

"He never mentioned it."

"I suppose she gave it away."

"Well, I wouldn't want to have to start married life with that bird squawking at me."

"You had to start married life with me."

"That's right." He gives my hair a gentle tug. "You can get used to anything. Not so much squawking out of you as that parrot, though."

We are at the corner of Garden Street and Chauncy. "Shall we cut over to Mass Av and catch the trolley or walk home?" Pat's counting the change in his hand to see if we have carfare. The Chevy's broken down, for the last time, I guess. It's a long way uphill, up Garden and Sherman, but for some reason I feel like the walk.

"I hope there's beer in the icebox," Pat says. "Old man Gallagher was pretty stingy with the booze."

"That's why there wasn't a riot."

"Well, you know, I don't much care about riots any more." We are looking into the hardware-store window. Pat has been pricing drill sets. "I'll miss Gowan, Maureen."

"So will I."

We walk some more. The sidewalk is frosted and slippery under our feet. Pat says, "They pull out a tooth, you feel around for it with your tongue for a while, then you get used to the hole. There are too many other things to think about."

I take his arm. Over the railroad tracks, across Rindge, up Montgomery, to the corner of Winter Street.

"She made a pretty bride."

"Nowhere near as pretty as you."

Oatmeal for breakfast. Coarse flakes fall into the water, thicken, bubble again to the surface. My tears salt the oatmeal in the pan. The stored-up grief is gone. I don't know why.

In April there is a freeze and the oak leaves, still clinging to the trees from last year, are encased in ice. Pat's going down the back steps, off to collect Angela, who has been having supper with his mother. Tomorrow is Angela's second birthday. I grab my coat from the hook by the door and run after him down the stairs. "I'll go with you."

The neighborhood kids are outside playing hide-and-seek in the dark. You can't see them, but you hear their high-pitched voices: allee, allee, allee, in-come-free. Could be Cissy and me. Soon it will be Angela, tearing toward home base, crafty and passionate about a game.

Walking past the French Church, Pat and I hear faint sounds of organ music. We go around to the side door to see if it is unlocked; the door is heavy, but Pat pushes it open. I pull a wrinkled scarf out of my coat pocket and tie it over my hair.

The church is empty and unlit, except for a few frail candles near the altar. The plaster saints are quiet, without expression, thoughtful perhaps. Our fingers and foreheads are wet with Holy Water; we dip our knees, in a less perfunctory way than usual, and cross ourselves.

The organist, high up under the rafters, shuffles his music sheets. This is only practice. He makes a few false starts and then there is a violent confusion of sound, echoing from every cranny and chink in the stone walls.

Pat kneels beside me in the pew. I wonder what his prayers are like. His face is calm. His forehead is higher than I ever noticed before and his shoulders more rounded, all those years of bending over people's feet. He looks like his father, of course, and yet not like him at all.

Dense fugal noise inhabits everything; even the candles vibrate and flicker. It blots out everything. I am not able to pray. The music stops with a short high whine from the organ, and the organist flicks off his light and leaves through some secret side door.

Outside, the trucks are barreling out Rindge Avenue toward Route Two and a fire-engine siren screeches somewhere. Probably the trash chutes in the public housing going up again.

"Pat, I have to tell you something." We stand in the churchyard. The sky is dark now, flecked randomly with stars; I can't pick out the constellations. He's waiting for me to say my piece, and I suppose the confession may as well be blunt. "I was pregnant when you married me."

"I know."

"I mean, not with your baby."

"I know that, too. Remember the first time Gowan had us down to the beach house? After you went to bed

Gowan and I got drunk. He told me he thought you were in trouble."

"That's a quaint way of putting it."

"I got the idea."

"Then you married me out of pity."

"No." He sounds surprised. "I grabbed my chance. I figured you wouldn't have me otherwise."

"Why not?"

He shrugs. "Well, I still don't please you, do I?"

"That's my own stupid fault."

"Doesn't matter whose fault."

"You know something, Pat? Everyone I've ever loved has gone away from me, one way or another. Even you."

"I didn't get very far, did I? Only to the bus terminal, and a ton of snow dumped on me." We both laugh quietly. Then he says all of a sudden, "Maureen, things are going to be better now."

"Yes."

We walk together over to Verdun Street, hurrying because of the cold. April, but a long time until spring.